A Time
To Dream

A Time
To Dream

RUTH GLOVER

Beacon Hill Press of Kansas City
Kansas City, Missouri

Copyright 1995
by Beacon Hill Press of Kansas City

ISBN 083-411-5727

Printed in the
United States of America

Cover illustration by Keith Alexander

Library of Congress Cataloging-in-Publication Data

Glover, Ruth.
  A time to dream / Ruth Glover.
    p.   cm.—(The Wildrose series; bk. 3)
  ISBN 0-8341-1572-7 (pbk.)
  1. Frontier and pioneer life—Saskatchewan—Wildrose—Fiction. 2. Women pioneers—Saskatchewan—Wildrose—Fiction. 3. Wildrose (Sask.)—History—Fiction. I. Title. II. Series: Glover, Ruth. Wildrose series; bk. 3.
PS3557.L678T56   1995
813'.54—dc20

                                                              95-43066
                                                              CIP

10   9   8   7   6   5   4   3   2

To my three brothers, who
share my poignant memories of
the log parsonage in
Saskatchewan's bush country—
Fred, Bud, and Al Vogt

ABOUT THE AUTHOR

Ruth Vogt Glover knows well the hardships women faced on the Western frontier of North America. She recalls that her mother, Queena Vogt, owned only one good dress and worked long hours in and around the family's home near Macdowall, deep in the bush country of central Saskatchewan. Winters were long and confining, sandwiching short summers of harried, intense labor.

"Like so many of the women who lived in the area, my mother came from a more genteel home—she was raised in Winnipeg—before moving to the raw bush," Mrs. Glover explains. "Such women were true pioneers in many ways. Leaving what were usually better conditions, they came into the area and endured great deprivation while showing tremendous courage and hardiness. Many of them left just about everything behind."

For more than a decade Mrs. Glover's father, Harry F. Vogt, was minister of the small country congregation who met in the district's schoolhouse. It was this schoolhouse that formed the model for the one in this novel and her previous ones—*The Shining Light* and *Bitter Thistle, Sweet Rose*. The Vogt family lived in a log parsonage nearby.

Mrs. Glover and her husband, Hal, currently live in The Dalles, Oregon, where he pastors a church and she pursues her writing. The Glovers revisited central Saskatchewan most recently in the summer of 1994 with one of Mrs. Glover's brothers, Bud, and his wife. Although the ongoing cutting-away of the bush made it a challenge to get their bearings, Mrs. Glover said, many of the old landmarks remain—including the old schoolhouse—and the group enjoyed finding them and visiting with relatives.

Mrs. Glover has written extensively for a number of Christian periodicals. *A Time to Dream* is her third novel.

1

WHY DOESN'T HE HUSH? CASSIE THOUGHT FRET-
fully. I can't hear the meadowlark!

Cassie deemed it very important to hear the meadowlark. After all, its song had been the voice of promise,
always calling across the endless prairies as she and Rob
followed its invitation to dreams yet unfulfilled. How often, hearing its lilting melody, they had sought each other's eyes with a smile, a nod, and a lifting of tired shoulders! Mile after wearying mile they had put behind them,
in response to the meadowlark's summons.

"A time to be born, and a time to die," the voice was
saying.

To Cassie, standing across the open grave, the words
came and went as though from a great distance or as if
muffled through a winter quilt pulled over her head.

A time to be born she could understand. Even now the
child, hers and Rob's, struggled within her body, restless
until freed—freed to a life she and Rob had planned for it
in the wideness of the West, a place where horizons were
of your own making and dreams came true.

That Rob's dream and hers should now be tumbled into a dark hole in the endless prairie was unthinkable. Only
yesterday they had encouraged each other . . .

"Rest now," she had told her husband gently, alarmed
in spite of herself by his flushed cheeks and labored breath,
and he had responded as he so often had, "We'll make it,

sweetheart—you and I and Robin." For that was the name he had picked for the baby—boy or girl.

But Rob wouldn't make it! The realization skimmed the surface of Cassie's mind without being real; it couldn't be so.

There had been ominous signals along the way, but in her blind optimism Cassie had refused to face them. Each "spell" had left Rob thinner and more hollow-eyed. But he had always insisted on pressing on; at times he had even stepped up the pace, as though hurrying to meet some time schedule.

"I've had these problems for years," he would say when Cassie urged a rest upon him. "I've always gotten over them—you watch and see."

But Cassie remembered the warnings of Ma Bates, the kindly neighbor who had taken Rob into her home when he was 10, after his parents died.

"Go if'n you have to, Robbie," Ma had said, sighing, "but take keer. Remember—you have a weak chest. Can cold snowdrifts be any better for you than the cornfields of Ioway?"

But Robbie couldn't be happy until he had an outfit ready for the long haul and had put a ring onto Cassie's finger. Young, eager, and optimistic, Rob and Cassie Quinn had joined the band of immigrants who—land-hungry and wooed by the promise of "the cheapest and also some of the best land in the world"—were converging on the vast Northwest Territories.

All that land free for the taking! One hundred sixty acres—for a 10-dollar filing fee!

Not considered by most of them was the stipulation that they clear 10 acres a year for three years or, harder still, that they live on their holding for six months out of each year. Many found the price too high. Even now Rob and Cassie met families trudging the way of retreat and defeat, overcome by the endless trees to be removed, stumps to be grubbed, summer's dreadful heat, winters so cold the mercury dropped to the bottom of the thermometer and stayed there for days at a time, plagues of mosquitoes, unendurable isolation in a soddy or dugout, and only rare contact with a doctor.

For those who stayed, often the first "crop" was buffalo bones. In the spring the prairie seemed abloom with white drifts of them. For the enterprising, income was augmented by hauling the bones to the railroad, where they could be sold for about seven dollars a ton.

And so they endured—some of them. It was possible! That Rob and Cassie would be happy homesteaders they never questioned. Their dreamland, however, lay beyond the prairies. The bush, or parkland, drew them—with the siren song of a meadowlark.

The oxen were desperately slow, trying the patience of Rob in particular. A day's travel of 20 miles—possible for horses—was beyond the oxen. And if they came to a creek, the stubborn creatures fell to their knees, resisting all efforts to rise, until the wagon was unloaded and everything carried across.

Nevertheless, Rob had urged his plodding animals to their utmost ability, walking alongside most of the way, at times draping netting over their heads when mosquitoes threatened to drive them, headstrong, into a slough for relief. ("Oho! Not reluctant to enter the water now, you stubborn beasts!")

Cassie had dreamed the days away, riding the jolting, springless wagon without complaint, walking with Rob, or wandering the prairie to gather flowers. She had happily coped with limited supplies, soiled clothes, and what seemed like unending miles. To have Rob put his arms around her and pull her close at night in their blanket nest under the wagon, feel the cooling breeze on her cheek, and, eventually, press a hand to the new life growing within her body was enough to send her drifting into a night of sweet rest, filled with sweeter dreams.

It was at Winnipeg, gateway to the West, that Rob had succumbed to the first bad bout with his "weak chest." "Quinsy," the bleary "doctor" had announced before taking their money and departing. And soon Rob, restless and driven, had insisted they move on. "We've got to get to Prince Albert," he had said doggedly.

For years York boats had plied the Saskatchewan River. Red River carts had creaked overland. Following the defeat of the Métis after their abortive uprising under Riel, and with a strong show of mounted police billeted in the area, the Saskatchewan West received good press in the United States and abroad, and the trickle of immigrants, soon to swell to tens of thousands, had started in earnest.

But almost impassable roads were a deterrent; farmers, needing to sell their crop, spent many weeks on the trails hauling their grain. Clearly it was imperative to get the railroad into the North.

When in 1890 the first train reached Prince Albert, a grand celebration was planned, with advertising luring the public: "Prince Albert and the Northern Saskatchewan: A Guide to the Fertile Belt now being opened up by railway from Regina to Prince Albert, the Central City . . . of Saskatchewan."

And the wagons had trekked north in spite of the rails, Rob Quinn's among them. Though small in comparison to some, it had been carefully loaded. Rob had bypassed Regina, formerly called "Pile of Bones," and they labored on, ever northward. More than once the wagon trains they joined moved on while Rob struggled with his cough and his pain until he was able to drive.

Until last night.

A time to die Cassie couldn't comprehend—certainly not at the side of a rude soddy where strangers slept the night away! Not coughing one's life blood into the grasses of a prairie! And not until your children and grandchildren had grown content in the fulfillment of your dream for them!

Dying—going into the sunset—had seemed distant in time and planning and was to be faced hand-in-hand with Rob when the sunrise was behind them. Now the hot sun blazed overhead, and Rob had not reached his noonday. Cassie's head thrummed with the pictures that thrust themselves upon her, to fade as quickly and silently as they came.

"A time to weep, and a time to laugh," said the speaker—whether a preacher or someone drafted for the occasion, Cassie never knew. His words demanded tears; Cassie had none. Her eyes were as dry as the sod under her feet, her heart as empty as the vast sky overhead. Would she ever laugh again?

"A time to get, and a time to lose; a time to keep, and a time to cast away . . . a time to love . . . a time of peace."

Laughter was gone; love was gone; embracing was over and done. With the terrible finality of it all came peace.

Peace and Rob's legacy: a homestead in the bush for Robin.

2

"YEP, IT'S COMING, ALL RIGHT. AND RIGHT ON THE button!" The Meridian stationmaster made the announcement from a kneeling position, his ear plastered to the humming rail and his vigorous mustache all but sweeping the cinders.

Even as he dusted the knees of his pants, townsfolk could be seen coming from the doorways of the few buildings that made up the small hamlet, converging on the raw building beside the gleaming railroad tracks. The excitement generated by the arrival of the train was almost as gripping as a visit by a traveling salesman with his supply of goods from the "outside" or the once-a-month appearance of the doctor from Prince Albert.

Before the train was seen, it was heard, shrieking its greeting above the verdant growth that had been painstakingly hacked back to clear a path for its invasion of the bush country. And none too soon for these isolated pioneers. As testimony of the benefit the train offered, several cream cans stood ready for loading. Across the tracks countless cords of wood were stacked, always needed by the belching monsters that were threading the Northwest Territories, and the sale of which brought much-needed income to families whose few cleared acres could not supply their needs. Yes, life was better for the people of the parkland with the advent of the railroad.

Today was more interesting than usual. As a passenger alighted with what, even to the most unimaginative watcher, was a queenly air, the eyes of every male in town were drawn for a brief, tantalizing moment to a very shapely ankle and an expensive shoe on which shone a japanned buckle.

Even the most ignorant among them recognized the elegance of the concoction perched atop the small head around which a few dark red curls strayed, no doubt in wanton disregard of last-minute efforts to conclude the wearying journey as properly as possible. And every observer determined to entertain the family at the supper table with a detailed description of it: "You'd have to see it to believe it! It was straw—but all around here," and work-worn fingers circled heads of damp, freshly slicked down hair, "was a puff of net, sort of pinned down with ah—rosettes, I guess you'd say. And here and there—" calloused fingers jabbed the air here and there, "were loops of ribbon—*satin* ribbon." Here words failed, and only a shake of a masculine head conveyed the effect of the amazing headgear.

After a few moments of awed silence in deference to it, the narrative was resumed: "And her shoes—you should have seen those shoes! Pointed as all get-out!"

And more than one fascinated housewife or grown daughter tucked her worn, round-nosed boots under the supper table as she pictured in her mind the stylish footwear.

"Could rival a hat pin for staving off unwelcome advances," the men continued, and the womenfolk nodded knowing heads, murmuring, "Probably the new coin toe. Some call it the quarter toe because it's about the width of a 25-cent piece. What color were they?"

"Well, ah—dark red—wine, I guess you'd say."

"Oxblood."

Hungry for any tidbit of news in their otherwise usual day of unrelenting dawn-to-dark workload and far removed from the fashions of the day—except as featured in the newspapers that filtered through to them or the magazines that were sent in batches by some distant relative— their concept of "fashion" was obtained from the ubiquitous catalog, bible of the backwoods. The coin toe, or the equally new opera toe or needle toe, with tips, was the cause of much curiosity.

"Maybe I'll get to see them," wives said wistfully. "Go on—what else was she wearing?"

"Well, ah—she wore a cape."

"What color? What style?"

"Well, ah—just a cape—"

"But was it fancy silk? Imported English? Trimmed with lace or grosgrain? Overlaid with straps? Pearl-buttoned? Was it lined with figured silk or changeable taffeta?"

"Well, ah—" The men, caught in coils of their own making, fumbled. "It was all very tasteful—nothing you wouldn't approve of—"

"You saw just the hat and shoes, I suppose!" women said scathingly.

"She was a neat package—I can say that," more than one husband finished appreciatively and then wondered why his wife's eyes turned frosty.

Aloud, they defended themselves. "After a few words with Rudy, she went on into the waiting room." How to describe the sharp tapping of the small shoes or the swishing of the skirt? To mention the skirt was to open a whole new line of questions: color? material? four-yard sweep? rustle-lined? The males of the district quailed and quieted.

"Waiting for the preacher," wives were saying knowingly.

"The—preacher?"

"Gerald Victor," wives explained patiently. "Everyone was discussing it last Sunday. Brother Victor's cousin was expected from London, Ontario."

"Mighty long way to come just to see a cousin."

"That's what we all thought—especially a cousin you haven't seen since you were a child. We suspect there's something behind it. Even the Victors don't know why a girl—"

"Woman."

"A *female* would come so far unless there is some good reason. After all, it's no picnic here."

And many a couple fell silent, reliving the bitter workload and the bitterer elements of this their chosen home.

Rallying, husbands eventually said, "Good luck to the Victors as they entertain her royal highness! Now—can we eat?"

Men! thought the women fondly and passed the fried potatoes.

* * *

Stepping to the platform in her Sicilian silk cape and her black brilliantine skirt, Meredith Deane's gaze swept the ring of watching faces. Friendly, sympathetic, curious— but it was clear no one was stepping forward to meet her.

Getting a fresh grip on the roomy Boston shopping bag she carried in one hand and tucking the magazine she had been reading more firmly under her arm, she turned to Rudy Bannister, who was overseeing the loading of the cream cans.

"Excuse me, my good man," she said in a clear, well-modulated voice, "but can you tell me if Gerald Victor is among these—persons standing here?"

"Nope."

"You mean you can't tell me, or he isn't here?"

Turning from his task, Rudy's gaze widened as he took in the vision before him, from the aforementioned hat to the tapered shoes and all the attractions in between.

"Oh, s'cuse me, Miss," he said apologetically, doffing his hat. "The answer is yes, I can tell you, and no, he isn't here."

The pointed toe tapped, and the gray eyes turned a trifle anxious as the young woman scanned the hamlet's scattered buildings.

"I don't suppose there's a place," she said tentatively, "where a person could get a room—"

"If I were you, Miss," Rudy said kindly, "I'd just go into the waiting room and er—wait. He'll be here; you can count on it. Trouble is, we had a big rain last night, and roads—just lanes, most of them—are apt to be quagmires in places. Things are pretty raw here in the bush, Miss. But the preacher is dependable—he'll be here."

Meredith cast a look at the sun, beginning its slide toward the west, and, throwing back her cape, snapped open a heavily engraved watch that was fastened to a waist of the finest-quality French lawn. Before she closed it, Rudy's eyes glimpsed, in the watch's cap, the handsome face of a man.

"Thank you," she said, drawing the cape around her slim form again. "I will do as you suggest. No doubt my cousin will be here shortly."

But she was filled with some trepidation as she seated herself on a hard bench, trying again to fit her aching body to unyielding wooden arms. Her baggage, she noted, had been stacked in a tidy pile outside the door.

Having spent all of 30 seconds acquainting herself with Meridian's length and breadth and noting how it was enclosed in the grip of the bush, Meredith turned her attention elsewhere. Reaching for the publication she had been reading on the train, she thumbed quickly.

She knew what she was looking for. It was a quotation from Shakespeare—or so the *Youth's Companion* claimed. Whoever was responsible for writing it,' reading it had brought a catch to her breath and a sharp pain to her heart.

The large publication, more a newspaper than a magazine, was designated the "New England Edition." New England, and here she was in the far and distant West! Yet not so distant but what the paper and the pain had accompanied her—through dense forests, across endless prairies, and into the depths of the bush—present, bitter companions. Leaning her head against the wall (carefully, because of the hat), Meredith closed her eyes as memories, uninvited and unwanted, crowded past the barriers she had deliberately erected and trampled the wound once again.

All unbidden, a portion of Scripture rose in her thoughts: "Whither shall I flee from thy presence?" Consoling, if one were applying it to the abiding presence of a faithful God; but tormenting when one recognized an obviously unsuccessful flight from someone less—far less—constant.

With these dark thoughts, Meredith opened her eyes and read again the couplet. It was titled "Profitless Grief."

To mourn a mischief that is past and gone
Is the next way to draw new mischief on.

It's really just another way of saying, "Let bygones be bygones," I suppose, she thought. Easier said than done, as indicated by her present turmoil.

But honesty prevailed, and Meredith admitted to herself, Perhaps I'm not mourning the mischief half so much as I'm just plain—exercised about it!

Reluctantly she pondered the mix of hurt, humiliation, and rejection that had prompted her flight from Ontario and the luxurious offices of Brandt Bros. Textiles—and from the arms of Emerson Brandt.

Just thinking about Emerson reminded her of his male ego, and it spiraled Meredith into an agitation that sent hot blood warming her cheeks. No doubt her eyes flashed, because Rudy Bannister, who had stuck his head into the doorway, looked startled and hastily withdrew.

"Arrogant—supercilious—chauvinistic male!" Meredith was spluttering to herself.

Feeling a little better after her outburst at the absent Emerson, and still seeing no sign of an approaching male figure bent on locating someone he probably wouldn't recognize, Meredith turned to the publication again.

It seemed the *Youth's Companion* was celebrating its 71st birthday by promising its readers that in 1897, the upcoming year, the magazine would contain "many exceptionally brilliant features." She noted with annoyance that, of the 35 names on "The Brilliant Roll of Our Contributors," only 5 were female.

Emerson would feel so smugly reinforced! Recalling her last conversation with him, Meredith all but gnashed her teeth in frustration.

That the "roll" included such gentlemen as Hon. Henry Cabot Lodge, Rev. Edward Everett Hale, D.D., Andrew Carnegie, Lieutenant R. E. Peary, U.S.N., and Rudyard Kipling impressed her not one whit! Where were the notable women?

Interest was stimulated in Lieutenant Peary's article, "Hunting Musk Ox Near the Pole," by telling how "some explorers saved themselves from dying of hunger by a desperate charge upon these 'Elephants of the North.'"

Kate Chopin's contribution, however, titled "Aunt Lympy's Interference," was introduced by—"A romantic little story, charmingly told, of a self-reliant Creole girl, a rich uncle, an indignant old family servant, and a bashful young planter whose fence got out of repair suspiciously often."

"Pure treacle!" Meredith muttered. "Why won't they let us women say something worthwhile?"

And sitting in a raw railroad station surrounded by hardworking pioneers whose main attention was given to sheer survival, Meredith fanned the flames of her campaign for equality of the sexes.

Now this ought to be interesting, she said to herself and folded back the paper to the article titled "The Real 'New Woman.'" Whether written by a man or a woman, the paper did not reveal. Probably a woman, she decided when the author began by showing a degree of sympathy toward the "widespread advance of women within recent years."

She changed her mind when the writer objected to the use of the phrase "new woman." The *man* stated, "Men are too well-contented with womanhood as it has been, to welcome a change involving any radical departure from the ideals of the past."

Emerson personified!

"The phrase 'the new woman,'" the know-it-all declared, "suggests the cartoons of the comic papers. One thinks of bloomers and other semimasculine experiments in dress; of unfeminine voices; of various grotesque assumptions of the place and power that belong to a man."

Shades of Emerson Brandt!

"Bosh! Stuff and nonsense!" Meredith gritted in a most unfeminine voice.

How could Emerson be so against a concept to which she, Meredith, was so dedicated? If he truly loved her—

Mightily frustrated at what she considered Emerson's betrayal—and he a thousand miles away, in body as in philosophy—Meredith whipped aside her cape, grasped the gold-encased watch, snapped it open, and stuck out her tongue at the arrogant, handsome face that stared back at her.

"Pardon me—but are you all right?"

Meredith raised startled eyes to the face bending near her own, a masculine face, its naturally dark countenance made darker still by concern. Snapping the watch shut, Meredith managed, "Oh, er—ah—just dry throat—" and her voice squeaked embarrassingly.

Meredith allowed the tip of her tongue to touch her lips ever so daintily, despising herself at the same time for the subterfuge. But to be caught in a display of such childishness! Would Cousin Gerald accept her faltering excuse? Or was he laughing at her?

But it was with a straight face the man said, "It's been

a very long trip. I'm sure you're parched. Perhaps Muller's —the store across the road—will have some cherry phosphate or something like that."

"No, no," Meredith interjected quickly. "I'm fine now —truly I am. I'd rather we just get on our way, if you don't mind."

"Of course. You must be tired. It really means a great deal that you came. Mother is especially happy about it. She'll have a meal ready—"

"Mother?"

"She can't do much, of course," the man explained, "but at least you won't have to do anything tonight. Tomorrow when you're rested—"

"Mother?" Meredith repeated again, gropingly. "Your mother is here?"

"Why, of course." The man's eyes were puzzled. "I thought you understood that. I wouldn't have agreed to your coming if she wasn't here. I'm sure you understand— the proprieties and all that."

As he spoke, he helped Meredith to her feet, handing her the discarded *Companion*, urging her toward the door.

Her elbow in his grip, Meredith obeyed.

On the platform he indicated her mound of luggage— matching alligator leather Gladstone bags, a handsome canvas case bound with wide leather and with heavy corner protectors, a club bag or satchel, and a trunk.

"Are these yours?" he asked in a strangled voice.

"It's not much, really," defended Meredith quickly, catching what seemed a note of dismay in the man's reaction. "I brought some books—I knew you'd like that—and some presents for the family. And, of course, my own wardrobe and personal things—I don't know how long I'll stay, so some of the clothes were included for colder weather—"

"Presents? There's certainly no need for presents. Your pay, I'm afraid, will be inadequate at best—"

"Pay? Of course, I expect to do my share—but pay? Why," and Meredith laughed lightly, "just a hug and kiss from time to time will be ample, thank you!"

And when her companion seemed startled, Meredith's laugh trilled more merrily.

"And by the way," she said, looking up into the masculine face above her, "where's my welcome hug and kiss? Really, my dear, I didn't suppose you had turned into a prude just because you're a—"

"Your dear?"

"Well, you *are* a dear, you know. I always think of you fondly."

The dark man's face turned darker yet.

"I think we had better discuss our arrangement before we go any further," he said stiffly.

"Gerald, Gerald," Meredith clucked, grasping the man's arm and giving it a shake, "I do believe you've turned into a stick-in-the-mud! Now where's that kiss?"

"Gerald?" the man repeated blankly.

"You—you're—not—Gerald?"

3

THROUGH THE DOOR OPEN TO THE EVENING breeze, Cassie could only imagine the distant mound of drying prairie soil and its covering of limp wildflowers.

Mrs. Ramsey dipped a ladle into the rabbit stew simmering in an iron pot and brought a steaming bowl to Cassie.

"Eat, my dear," she said kindly, and when Cassie hesitated, added, "If not for you, then for the baby." Cassie ate.

As though the day and its sorrow had sapped them of vitality, three children emptied their bowls and crept like field mice into dark corners of the soddy to sleep.

Mr. Ramsey's heavy boots ground through the prairie earth, bringing the milk from the barn—a replica of the house, both of them carved from their own land and piled around them for protection and warmth.

The homesteader's wife rinsed the strainer in water that had been hauled, Cassie knew, from the sliver of green growth at the foot of the distant hills; the gaunt man picked up his bowl from the table, along with a hunk of bread, and seated himself.

His voice was gentle and his sigh was real as he spoke: "It's a hard way to end it all—far, far from home."

Cassie looked up in surprise. "But—we have no other home," she said. "Neither of us. Rob was an orphan; my grandmother raised me until her health failed and then gladly put me in Rob's charge."

"You mean you have no family—nobody to go back to?"

"No one."

"I see." Mr. Ramsey's tone was thoughtful.

"Our home for—oh, I guess it's been six months—has been our wagon. Everything we own is in it. We wintered back in the States. Rob helped a sheepherder, and we shared his shack. With the first sign of spring, we were on our way again."

"Heading for the bush, you say?"

"Rob's friend, Mike Barber, is working in Prince Albert. We were heading to his place, and from there—a homestead."

"You're not the first to be sidetracked. That little cemetery is filling up fast. Maybe you noticed."

Cassie hadn't.

"Have you thought what you'll do, Mrs. Quinn? You are more than welcome to stay with us—" Mrs. Ramsey's voice, though kind, was hesitant, as though aware that their accommodations were unfit for their own needs, let alone a guest.

"I couldn't possibly," Cassie said and heard Mrs. Ramsey's small sigh of relief, "though I thank you."

"People come through all the time, heading back out." The lady continued her train of thought concerning Cassie's uncertain future. "You can wait right here until you can latch onto someone."

Cassie hesitated.

"Or—you can go on to Duck Lake. Mr. Ramsey could take time to see you that far. You'll fare better near people."

"I don't think—"

"Well, my dear, don't worry about it tonight. 'Sufficient unto the day,' you know. There *are* other options." Mrs. Ramsey's eyes sought her husband's in a look that was significant.

With the dawn, or very soon after, Cassie's first "option" appeared. It appeared in a worn wagon containing a haggard man and four weary children. Cassie wondered at what hour they had stumbled from their beds; the bright sun shone on red-rimmed eyes, uncombed hair, and tired faces.

"Jeremiah, glad to see you. Get down and come on in." Mr. Ramsey had hurried from the barn to the sound of the rig, and he reached a hand to the children, who tumbled from the wagon and stood, sad and somehow so alone that Cassie's heart went out to them.

Apparently Mrs. Ramsey's heart did likewise. "Come —there's breakfast for all."

The eyes brightened, and the children made their way shyly toward the soddy. From it erupted the Ramsey children, and after a few hesitant starts, conversation was off and running. Cassie took the bowls Mrs. Ramsey filled from the pot of oatmeal they had eaten of earlier and set them in front of the newcomers.

The doorway was darkened by the entrance of Mr. Ramsey and Jeremiah. "Jeremiah Dubray," Mr. Ramsey said. "And this, Jeremiah, is Mrs. Quinn."

Jeremiah's huge hand gripped Cassie's, and his frank blue eyes studied Cassie's face with honest concern.

"I heard about your grief, Ma'am," he said. "Sure am sorry."

"Thank you."

Jeremiah sat at the table with his children and quickly swallowed a large bowl of cereal, followed by several slices of bread.

"I don't get baking like this often, Sarah," he said, "so I know you'll excuse me."

Mrs. Ramsey nodded, smiled, and passed the platter.

Pouring coffee for all four adults, Mrs. Ramsey urged Cassie to a seat beside the table and joined her guests and her husband.

"Jeremiah farms about 12 miles east of us," Mr. Ramsey explained. Twelve miles! The poor man and the poorer mites had been on the road since goodness-knew-when.

The men talked of crops and weather. Cassie pleated the edge of the tablecloth (fancy it—a tablecloth in the barbaric living conditions of a raw homestead on the prairie, and though wrinkled, white as snow!) and lost herself in the immediacy of her problem and the desperation.

"Poor man," Mrs. Ramsey was saying in a low voice, indicating Jeremiah by a small jerk of her head in his direction.

Poor man? Cassie looked curiously at the visitor and found him big, healthy, soft-spoken. Aside from a somewhat rumpled, careless appearance—certainly understandable considering his long drive—he seemed undeserving of pity.

But Mrs. Ramsey was continuing: "Millie, his wife, died about five months ago. Her grave is also out there where—" Mrs. Ramsey's nod in the direction of the cemetery was expressive.

Cassie's wounded heart felt the pain of another's sorrow. "Poor man," she whispered compassionately and looked at the stranger with new eyes. What he must be enduring—clinging to his dream and his future, alone.

But his problem was more serious. Cassie thought of the children playing outside, stretching weary legs before the long trip home. Motherless children . . .

Nevertheless, she was taken aback when Mr. and Mrs. Ramsey, with nods to each other, drifted from the soddy, Mrs. Ramsey to a mighty clashing of the morning's milk pails and Mr. Ramsey to disappear in the direction of the chicken yard. Jeremiah stayed seated at the table, strangely silent. Finally, clearing his throat, his eyes fixed on the cup in his hand, he spoke.

"Mrs. Quinn, I surely do sympathize with—with what has happened to you. And I understand you're having a baby." The man's eyes, kind in his weather-darkened face, lifted to Cassie's.

There seemed to be no response necessary, so Cassie made none.

"Here on the prairie and in the bush, and wherever people are pioneering and homesteading, life doesn't always proceed like we planned. Things change, and we accept them and go on."

Cassie understood that.

The man shifted his position. "What I'm trying to say—"

Cassie looked at him, puzzled by his seriousness, wanting to help him if she could.

"Yes, Mr. Dubray?"

Jeremiah set the cup down, leaned his arms on the table, and lifted earnest eyes to Cassie. "I need—someone, more than I can say." The voice faltered momentarily. "You need someone—more than you know. Mrs. Quinn, I'm asking you to marry me."

Startled, Cassie's fingers, still pleating the tablecloth, jerked, and a cup rattled in its saucer.

"Oh, Mr. Dubray—I couldn't think of such a—an arrangement!"

Jeremiah Dubray sighed. His eyes were filled with pain, and his face was a dull red as he finished. "I don't expect you to love me, Mrs. Quinn—although, God willing, that would come. I'm asking—pleading, if you wish—on behalf of my children—and yours. I'd be a father to it, Mrs. Quinn. I don't have much to offer now, but one day," his voice lifted with the confidence that kept him going, "my place will be prosperous. This land is prized—" His zeal colored his life with hope.

Cassie found her voice. "I know all that, Mr. Dubray. And you're right. One day your descendants will bless you. And one day mine will bless me, if I do what I must. And it's not to stay on the prairie, Mr. Dubray."

The hopeful eyes of the man slowly dimmed to hopelessness. Leaning across the table, he put his hand over Cassie's and said, "I'll leave it there, Mrs. Quinn. I have to get back to my place and my work, but—please—think on what I've said. The offer stands."

Rising, Jeremiah Dubray clapped his hat onto his head, strode from the soddy, and called to his children. After a brief word with the Ramseys, the little family—seeming forlorn and lonely against the stretching horizon—trundled away.

Mrs. Ramsey's eyes were sympathetic when she came in and sat across from Cassie. "It's the way of life on the frontier, my dear. Time after time two families, each missing a parent, join forces. And most of them don't wait long. Often it's the only solution. And usually it works out."

The conversation was interrupted by the sound of jingling harness and rattling wheels. Cassie looked out the open door to see a dusty buggy approaching. In it were a lone man and two children.

Cassie's second option pulled to a halt in the yard.

"Send him on his way, Mrs. Ramsey," Cassie said desperately.

"But, my dear, what in the world shall you do?"

"Do, Mrs. Ramsey? Why, I'll do just what Rob and I set out to do—I'm going on."

4 ❀

HER HEART FILLED WITH THE DREADFUL POSSI-bility. "You're not Gerald?" Meredith repeated.

"And you're not Miss Janoski?"

"Miss Janoski? Indeed I'm not!"

"And I'm not Gerald."

"Not Gerald—oh!—" With a muffled squeak (this is beginning to be a habit, she thought wildly), Meredith dropped the corduroy-clad arm she had clutched while she offered her cheek for a kiss. She put her gloved hands to her flaming cheeks and closed her eyes—closed them to shut out the dark eyes in the dark face of the man, eyes that were filling with laughter.

"Why in the world didn't you say so in the first place?" she spat out, unreasonably, of course, as she opened her eyes to the man's laughter.

"And why are you going around impersonating Miss Janoski?"

Meredith gasped at the impertinence. "You, sir, spoke first! You approached me—a total stranger!"

"And you offered me—a total stranger—a kiss."

"But—," protested Meredith, noting her voice was threatening to squeak again, "I thought you were my cousin!"

"So you say—now."

"Oh! You're impossible! It is *I* who should question *your* motives. Where, pray tell, is this fictitious Miss Janoski?"

"Keeping company, I should think, with your fabricated Gerald."

Almost panting with indignation and embarrassment, Meredith's response was cut short by the apologetic voice of Rudy Bannister.

"Sorry to interrupt," he said, obviously not sorry at all. (What a suppertime topic *this* would make!) "But this telegram is for you, Dickson."

"Excuse me," the man called Dickson said elaborately and proceeded to scan the paper.

Muttering something that sounded like "You are inexcusable" but couldn't possibly have been—coming from a lady of her breeding—Meredith turned and paced the small platform, fuming at her faux pas and Dickson's high-handed response to it.

"Lout—oaf!" she muttered and exhausted her vocabulary, but not her irritation.

When another voice said tentatively, "Meredith?" she whirled sharply to find herself face-to-face with the somewhat familiar face of her cousin. With something close to hysteria, Meredith flung herself into Gerald Victor's arms.

"Gerald!" she said with such relief that he patted her back reassuringly.

"There, there," he said soothingly. "I'm terribly sorry I'm late. I wouldn't have caused you concern for anything."

Over Gerald's shoulder Meredith caught a glimpse of the grinning face of the man to whom she had earlier offered her cheek. Younger than Gerald, dark-haired where Gerald was turning gray, dark-eyed where all the Victors were gray-eyed, his teeth gleamed white as he stepped forward toward the reunion scene, smiling.

"I think, Gerald," he said, "I was about to kidnap your cousin. You see, I'm here to collect a lady with whom I've been corresponding about coming to help while Grandma is down with rheumatism. It seems I made a mistake—unfortunately for me, I'm sure!"

Meredith watched through narrowed eyes; undoubtedly the rogue would put her at a disadvantage at any moment. And he was continuing gallantly, "What a friendly, outgoing person she is! I feel like I know her very well—very well indeed."

"And I've never met your equal," Meredith said meaningfully, "Mr.—"

"Oh, I'm sorry," Gerald said, "but I thought you knew—this is Dickson Gray. Dickson, this is my cousin—first cousin once removed, actually—Meredith Deane."

When Dickson Gray bowed over the proffered hand, an onlooker would have thought it was to hide a wicked gleam in his deep-set black eyes.

"Miss Deane expressed herself—quite picturesquely, I might add—as being quite—er—dry. No doubt the trip was tiring."

When Meredith's eyes flashed at what seemed to Gerald Victor an inane topic of conversation, he looked puzzled. "Well," he said, "we've got to get off home. Elva will have supper ready."

"Seriously, Gerald," Dickson Gray said, turning to his pastor, "this has been quite a blow—the failure of Miss Janoski to come, I mean. The load on Gran is just too much, what with the housework and taking care of Jennie too."

"A little prayer works wonders, Dickson."

"You're right, of course. And that's just what we'll do—pray. Nice to have met you, Miss Deane. Enjoy your visit; perhaps you'll extend it into the—er—cold weather." And Dickson Gray strode toward his horse and rig.

"I can't imagine what's gotten into Dickson," Gerald said thoughtfully. "Ordinarily he's the most disciplined of people."

It was a description that would have elevated anyone else in Meredith's eyes. "Disciplined" was the word that best of any described Mr. Emerson Brandt of Brandt Bros. Textiles Business.

And Emerson would have preened at the compliment. Emerson seemed to accept all his other attributes complacently: handsome, well-built, meticulous in his grooming, intelligent—all were accepted as his rightful due.

But discipline! This had been Emerson's goal, and he had directed every effort toward its fulfillment. And in him discipline was admirable, or so Meredith had come to believe. Certainly it had hastened his advance over his less-disciplined brothers into a place very near the top of the business.

Emerson had risen from office boy to having complete charge of the offices, and his aging father looked fondly on this particular son's ambitions to become vice president. The discipline that Emerson demanded in himself he expected in his associates.

Meredith liked to think it was her sense of discipline that Emerson had first found attractive in her. It was discipline that had prompted her to turn her back on the life of luxury provided by her uncle and aunt and insist on making her own way.

"But, Merry," they had expostulated again and again, "we love having you here—and what else do we have to spend our money on?"

"I know, dears," Meredith had responded fondly, "but I can't keep on taking and taking. Besides, women are beginning to find their place in the business world."

"We know all about that, dear. But it's getting a little bit out of hand, don't you think?" Meredith's aunt and uncle weren't entirely in favor of the "new woman." To them she seemed in danger of becoming bold, unladylike, even bossy. "Have you read tonight's paper, dear—the account of the brave woman who rebuked a brutal driver, shamed a crowd of indifferent men, and did it all with womanly dignity? You haven't? Homer, read it."

Clearing his throat, Uncle Homer had read how the driver of an overladen dray, drawn by four horses, began to beat them when they couldn't manage a sharp curve. A lady quietly took the whip from the driver's hand. Then, heedless of the man's curses, she stroked the necks of the horses and spoke kindly to them. The bystanders cheered and listened while the lady told the driver how to manage the horses, and the overloaded dray went on its way.

"Now this is the important part, dear," Uncle Homer had said gravely. "The correspondent of the *Transcript* sums it all up by saying, 'The aggressive party in this scene was not a "new woman," but one of gentle birth and breeding, with no sympathy with the "modern cult" of her sex.'"

"But Uncle," Meredith had insisted, "one can be part of the 'new woman' movement and continue being a lady!"

"Let us hope so," Uncle Homer had said skeptically while Aunt Marie looked doubtful.

Meredith felt confident she epitomized all things lady-like—until that undisciplined creature, Dickson Gray, taunted her into behavior definitely unacceptable; it didn't help her opinion of that male, and it certainly shook her confidence in her own much-prized self-control.

Even Emerson, at his most obnoxious, hadn't moved her from her display of discipline.

"You're wrong, Emerson, absolutely wrong," she had said coolly, head high, as she handed him his ring. "Let me know when you come to your senses."

And, as disciplined as she, Emerson had pocketed the ring.

Watching the departing buggy and the jaunty figure of Dickson Gray, Meredith wondered painfully what had happened to her carefully maintained discipline. How could she have allowed herself to sink to such a display of frivolous feminine humors?

"I hope it won't be necessary to socialize with that Dickson Gray," she said coldly.

"Socialize? We don't do much socializing in the bush, Cousin. But he is a near neighbor and a member of the church. I think," Gerald concluded thoughtfully, "he may have gotten off on the wrong foot."

"Oh, you mean he has another one?" Meredith asked tartly and clutched her hat as her cousin slapped the reins on the horse's rump. Off they moved, with a jerk, toward Wildrose.

5

"MISS DOVIE! MISS DULCIE!"

Dovie and Dulcie Snodgrass, hunched side by side in the rows of the garden, straightened aching backs and looked toward the road and the sound of the voice that hailed them.

"It's Dickson Gray," Dulcie said, shading her eyes.

"Comi-i-ing," warbled Dovie, dropping her hoe and hastening toward the waiting rig and driver. Dulcie, immediately behind her sister, seemed her exact shadow: sunbonneted and calico-gowned, their forms bustled almost in rhythm as they tripped lightly down the row.

"No hurry, girls," Dickson said, and the faces of the "girls" pinked with pleasure. "I picked up your mail when I was in town."

Dovie stepped on the lowest strand of barbed wire and pulled the higher string while Dulcie picked up her skirt, bent, and stepped through to the other side. She, in turn, separated the wires for her twin.

"How nice of you, Dickson!" Dovie said, reaching a dusty hand for the mail Dickson Gray was holding out to her—a few papers and one letter. Dovie's attention was given to the return address on the letter; reading it, her face fell.

"Thank you, Dickson," Dulcie said quickly. "But where is Miss—Janoski, is it? Shouldn't she be with you? I thought this was the day."

"It's the correct day, all right," Dickson Gray said with

a shrug of the shoulders, "but she wired that she wasn't able to make it. Not now at least."

"Ah, too bad. And just when you need her. Grandma Gray can hardly get around. And what with Jennie being such a little live wire and all."

"What will you do, Dickson?" inquired Dovie anxiously. "Do you have any other possibilities?"

"None," Dickson Gray said with a sigh. "As Brother Victor said, it's praying time."

"Of course! The good Lord will have a solution for you!" With relief the sisters turned the problem over to a Higher Power and went back to their garden, crawling through the barbed wire, turning and waving at their neighbor and pausing to glance at their mail before they resumed their work.

"From England," Dovie said, with a catch in her voice. "But not—"

"Not from Terence."

"Not this time," Dovie said.

"Dovie, if I've told you once I've told you—"

"A thousand times. Yes, I know, Sister. And still I keep on looking and expecting."

"But almost 20 years, Dovie!"

"Twice times 20, Dulcie, and I'll still look for it!"

"Oh, Sister," Dulcie said helplessly.

"The last thing he said to me—"

"I know, we all know, Anna and I and most everyone in Wildrose—'As soon as I get my mother settled, Dovie bird, I'll be over on the next boat.'"

"Those were his exact words."

"And his mother has been dead for 17 years. And his letters frittered out more than 14 years ago."

"Don't be cruel, Dulcie," Dovie whispered, her face stricken.

"I can't bear it, the way you keep watching, after all this time, for some word from Terence Amberly! We know he's alive. Friends write us that. We know he lives in the same place."

"We also know he has never married. And neither have I, Dulcie."

"Well, Sister, neither have I, and neither has Anna." Dulcie's kind tones softened her words. "And we've all been happy and busy, haven't we?"

"Ye-e-s, especially busy!" Dovie's face, youthful in spite of her nearly 40 years, dimpled. "And we better get on with it if we expect to eat this winter."

Once again the sisters bent to their task, as alike as two peas in the pods they were cultivating. Inseparable, only the advent of Terence had threatened any division.

Amid high cackling and much squawking, the sisters leaned on their hoes momentarily to watch Anna, their older sister, scattering grain to the chickens. Usually gracefully upright in spite of her "more than 40" years, Anna's shoulders seemed, to her sisters, to droop.

"She's working much too hard," Dulcie said uneasily.

"She seems to think she has to take care of us. And, of course, she always has." Dovie's voice was tender.

"Dear Papa's death is harder on her than on us, I believe—don't you, Sister?"

"She's being such a good soldier about it—stepping into Papa's shoes."

"In spite of us doing our best, she's working herself to death."

"We can't go on this way, Sister—we just can't."

The sisters fell silent. Then, as so often happened, they looked at each other, eyes alight with the identical idea, and spoke almost as one: "A man! What we need around here is a man!"

"Well, not for me, Dovie. I'm happy the way I am."

"And not for me, Dulcie. I have Terence to consider. No one could ever compare with Terence! I'm afraid I'll never be free to love again." Dovie heaved a massive sigh.

"Impossible, Dovie! It's an impossible dream. But if *I* can't consider marrying us a husband, and *you* won't—"

The blue eyes of the twins turned toward Anna.

"She won't take kindly to the suggestion," Dulcie said.

"We can't *tell* her, Sister!"

"You're right. We'll have to do it *for* her. But, Dovie, you and I are not really all that practiced in courtship, and to do it for someone else, well, I'm not sure."

"I know how it's done," Dovie said confidently. "After all, I'm experienced in matters of the heart. We'll do a sort of secondhand wooing."

"It will call upon all our resources, Sister. Do you really think it's the thing to do?"

"Absolutely! Our plight is desperate! We've simply got to have a man to replace dear Papa."

Dulcie capitulated. "You're right, Sister. Where do we start?"

"The very first thing to decide is 'who.'"

Two look-alike figures bent in earnest concentration over the turnips.

＊ ＊ ＊

Anna put a hand to her hair, usually confined in a neat bun at the nape of her neck but now wobbling loosely in its pins. Winding the long coil absently, twisting and pinning it firmly into place, her eyes strayed to the industrious efforts of her sisters.

Seeing Dulcie (or was it Dovie?) straighten and put a hand to what was obviously an aching back, Anna set down the empty pail and turned toward the house and the simmering teakettle. Mama had never forsaken the English custom of teatime, and though she had been gone more than five years, Anna carried on; Papa had appreciated it. And now, working as hard as they did, she and her sisters needed it. It gave them a much-deserved rest without an accompanying feeling of guilt and offered an opportunity for chitchat. They made it a rule not to talk about the farm and its problems at this special time. "It's a time to be ladies," Mama had insisted.

"After all," Mama had also said, "gentility is a matter of good manners." And so good manners prevailed in one isolated corner of Canada's vast territories.

Teatime, whenever possible, featured scones and, of course, tea. There were times across the years when tea leaves had been saved and reused until it took an active imagination to think of the brew as tea. But then another package would arrive from one of Mama's many sisters, and the ritual survived.

Now, pouring boiling water into the heated pot and settling a tea cozy over it, Anna set out a dish of pin cherry jelly—the finest the bush had to offer, in her opinion—and a bowl of fresh, sweet butter of her own churning. She removed from the big range's warming oven a covered plate of the revered scones.

Stepping outside the door, Anna sent the familiar call winging over the yard: "Teatime, girls!"

At a bench outside the door Dovie and Dulcie washed their hands and dashed cold, refreshing water onto their flushed faces—flushed not because of their exertions but because of their stimulation over the idea that had presented itself to them as a solution to their urgent need: Find Anna a husband!

Seated beside Mama's small parlor table, traditionally used for the tea ritual, Dovie and Dulcie studied their sister covertly. A fine figure of a woman, they concluded, and not a bit like them. They were built like the bush's chickadee, they admitted, small and round and, like the chickadee, given to bounciness. Anna, on the other hand, moved gracefully, was tall for a woman, and, though lined of face, could be called handsome.

Moreover, Anna was pure gold, a woman any man could be proud to call wife. Come to think of it, they would be doing a service not only for themselves but also for the man of their choice! What Anna would think of her impending nuptials they hadn't considered, though they did have a small, uncomfortable suspicion that their motives may not be the best.

But Anna would be happy about it—if they made the right choice for her. And so it was with expansive hearts Dovie and Dulcie opened their serviettes, spread them over their faded calicos, daintily spread butter and jelly onto their scones, and lifted fragile cups of fragrant tea to their pursed lips. (One never, never blew on her tea, Mama instructed.)

With a significant look at her twin, Dovie opened the conversation. "Dickson brought the mail—nothing special, just Aunt Celia's regular monthly letter." With an elaborate sigh, she added, "Poor Dickson."

"Poor Dickson?" repeated Anna, rising beautifully to the bait.

"Yes, poor man! He's been counting on that woman, a Miss Janoski, to come and help him with the house and all."

"She's not coming?"

"Can't make it. And Grandma Gray is getting badly twisted up with rheumatism. It's too much for her, doing all the work and looking after little Jennie too. You know, Sisters," Dovie said reflectively, "there's a situation as bad as ours, only in reverse. They need a woman in the home— we need a man. We have an abundance of women—"

"Perhaps you've hit on something, Dovie," Dulcie said with apparent surprise. "Perhaps we could combine households in some way."

"What Dickson needs," said practical Anna, checking the contents of the teapot, "is not three old maids cluttering up his place, but a wife."

The twins flashed expressive looks at one another; this was going better than they had dared hope.

"Oh, Anna, what a *wonderful* idea! Now that you've mentioned it, it's worth considering."

"You're too old for Dickson Gray, girls," Anna said dryly.

"Oh, Anna, what a dreadful thing to suggest, as if we—" Dulcie, flustered, defended herself. "Heavens! I'd never consider such a thing! And we all know Dovie is devoted to the memory of Terence!"

When Anna went to the kitchen to refill the pot, Dulcie and Dovie exchanged rueful glances.

"Well, Dickson is out—one down, two to go, I figure," Dulcie said.

"Morton Dunn and Digby Ivey, the only two bachelors in the district at the present time, unless we consider the Runyon brothers," Dovie said.

"Too old by far! After all, Sister, our purpose is to get someone to run the place, do the farming, the butchering, the shoeing, the—the—the—"

"The breeding," Dovie supplied, thinking of Bossy and the need for her to freshen next spring.

"That's what I was about to say!" Dulcie cried defensively. She was, after all, a farm girl—had been now for 20 years. But those early years of "gentility" in England had left their mark in many ways; Mama's mark never would be totally erased no matter how earthy bush life became.

"As for Morton Dunn," Dovie said thoughtfully, "I don't really fancy him as husband material."

"How do you feel about Digby Ivey, Sister?"

"I think I'd like him just fine," Dovie said slowly. "Of course, he's no spring—er—rooster either."

"I could accept Digby, I believe."

"That's settled then. We'll marry Digby."

"Of course, Digby has a son, don't forget. Would he object?"

"Shaver. What kind of name is that for a boy?"

"He's no boy, Sister. Must be all of 20. His folks called him their little shaver when he was small, and it's hung on. No doubt he'd be happy to have a mama after all these years. We'd get two for the price of one—Digby and Shaver!"

"What's this about Digby?" Anna asked, returning and setting down the teapot and resuming her place.

Dovie jumped, and what tea she had in her cup slopped into the saucer.

"Digging, Anna, digging! I'm quite worn out from digging!"

"We all are. That and all the other chores, not to mention the fact that the crop will soon have to be brought in."

"Poor dear Papa," Dulcie mourned. "Planted in good faith, never knowing he wouldn't be here to harvest."

The sisters wiped tears from their eyes with the corners of their serviettes.

"It's plain to see," Dovie said finally, "that we'll have to have help. Have you thought about it, Anna?"

"I've gone over the list of our neighbors in my mind, many times. The Ivey farm has two men on it. It's possible they could take on extra work."

"Anna!" both sisters shrilled, almost as one. "What a wonderful idea!" ("Poor innocent!" their rolling eyes said to each other. "Stepping right into the trap!")

"Someone will have to talk to them about it," Anna said. "They may take some persuading."

"Leave it to us, Sister!" Dulcie and Dovie chorused and clasped their hands in a positive excess of satisfaction.

6

THE FARMYARD CHURNED INTO A SEA OF MUD AS the wagons jostled for position. But the sun, rising over the distant line of the horizon, promised a change from the rains of the night—and a resumption of mosquito attacks, more than one lumpy-faced, insect-tormented pioneer thought gloomily. With final, shouted good-byes, three swaying prairie schooners pulled onto the rutted trail, heading north.

With a lump in her throat, Cassie rested her head momentarily on the shoulder of Mrs. Ramsey, feeling the comfort of arms around her once again and knowing these, too, must be abandoned.

"The grave—," she quavered.

"Yes, dear, we'll take care of it. Now up with you, or the wagon train you've waited for will be gone."

Mrs. Ramsey gave Cassie a final hug, the children clutched their mother's skirts and smiled shyly, and Mr. Ramsey, at the oxen's heads, waited her departure.

The prairie grasses brushed the sides of the trail, drying in the day's first warmth. To Cassie's eyes they appeared to stretch to infinity, broken only by the distant line of wagons ahead of her and behind her the small buildings, pathetic testimonies to man's brave attempt to conquer what had lain wild and free since time began.

The victory would not be won without casualties; just beyond the curve of the wide world, and fading fast from all but Cassie's memory, its latest victim lay, mute testimony of the prairie's domination.

"Rob—Rob—"

A wheel dipped into a gopher hole, startling Cassie from her final farewell. Thank God an ox had not stepped into the gaping tunnel! Cassie noted that her fellow travelers had continued to pull ahead, and she urged her plodders to a brisker pace.

Once again Cassie had to agree with Rob's oft-expressed regret concerning their thrift when purchasing their wagon. With only meager household goods and limited farming supplies to take with them, Rob had settled for a "narrow-track" wagon. Whereas the wide-track wagon measured five feet from tire to center; theirs measured four feet six inches. This meant that their rig did not run in the wider tracks of the bigger wagons, causing innumerable problems and slowing even further the already lumbering pace of their team of oxen—another economy.

Cassie took pride in her few possessions—Grandma's clock with its polished wood case of imitation black onyx, marbleized columns, and fancy bronze side ornaments; the heavy imitation cut-glass crystal fruit dish with the rococo base and ornamental handle, given to them as a wedding gift by Ma Bates; the "Complete Stove Furnishings Assortment" they had ordered, the list of which Cassie could still recite by heart: "one copper-bottom tin wash boiler, one teakettle, one cast-iron spider, one wrought-iron fry pan, one fire shovel, one four-pint tin teapot, one five-quart tin coffeepot, one 10-quart retinned dishpan, one revolving flour sifter, one biscuit cutter, one cake turner, one flat-handled skimmer," and more.

Rob had prized most of all, and wrapped against dents from shifting supplies, the Acme Air Tight Heating Stove ("burns woods, chips, or any offal"), guaranteed to keep a wood fire "overnight." The sturdy beauty of steel and planished iron ("usually called Russian iron"), advertised as the "most powerful heater for the least money," had just suited their dreams and their needs and would keep their first cabin warm and cozy.

In appreciation of the kindnesses shown by the Ramsey family, Cassie had rummaged through her boxes and pressed upon Mr. Ramsey such clothes she felt he could wear. She hesitated over Rob's coat, made of black duck with a heavy blanket lining, rubber interlined. Knowing she could no longer huddle under the oiled wagon cover during rain or biting wind, she had laid it aside for her own use. Now it lay on the wagon seat beside her; her hand strayed to it from time to time, caressing the sleeve still curved to the shape of Rob's arm and the corduroy collar worn from the rub of Rob's throat.

The beasts, perhaps dimly aware of a less-sure hand on the reins, moved at a more leisurely pace then usual; it was clear Cassie would make the journey more or less by herself. The other wagons were almost out of sight. Panic threatened.

Had she made the right decision? Thinking of it again, it once again seemed to be the only decision she could have made, aside from marrying some stranger. In Prince Albert she would locate Rob's friend, who was actually his foster brother—another orphan raised by Ma Bates. Who else did she have to turn to? No one, no one in the whole wide world. She felt very small and very frightened.

"Get up, you lazy critters!" The somnolent oxen jerked their heads in response to the command and the yank of the reins and quickened their steps.

＊　＊　＊

Cassie pulled into camp several hours after the others had called it a day.

Concerned men came to meet her, leading the oxen to a vacant place nearby, unhitching them and setting them to graze.

Kindly women helped Cassie, stiff and tired, from the wagon and led her toward the campfire. Having eaten, they prepared a plate of food for her.

"We lost sight of you early in the day," someone explained. "But we had an idea you'd keep on comin' until you found us." That is, unless you broke down somewhere along the way, more than one person thought. The possibility of it set more than one head shaking and lips to tightening.

Although she and Rob had slept under the wagon unless bad weather prohibited, Cassie cleared a place in the end of the wagon bed, spread her mattress and blankets, and prepared for sleep.

First, however, there was a call from Mr. Berger, who seemed to be in charge of the expedition.

"Mrs. Quinn, you're invited to join us for a few moments at the camp fireside."

Mrs. Berger swept her skirts aside, and Cassie, with Rob's coat around her shoulders, settled herself in the circle; even the children were quiet, some of them within the circle of their mothers' arms.

"It's our custom, Mrs. Quinn, to thank God for the mercies of the day and His watch care," Mr. Berger explained.

With this surprising announcement, he bent his bearded face over a small Book in his hands, leaning into the firelight to see.

"I'll read from Psalm 107 tonight," he said. "It reminds us how the Lord delivers His people from trouble—a reminder," he said, looking up with a smile, "that we all need from time to time.

"This portion is speaking of those that 'go down to the sea in ships.' I think it is fitting for us—" and Mr. Berger waved a hand toward the four prairie schooners looming over them, seemingly adrift in a sea of grass.

"Anyway," he continued, "these wayfarers, whether on land or sea, find their souls melted because of trouble."

That's me, Cassie thought with astonishment. That's exactly how I feel—melted because of trouble!

"'They reel to and fro,'" said the man, ". . . and are 'at their wit's end.'"

Me! That's me! He's describing me!

"'Then they cry unto the Lord in their trouble,'" Mr. Berger read, "'and he bringeth them out of their distresses. He maketh the storm a calm, so that the waves thereof are still . . . so he bringeth them unto their desired haven.'"

When Mr. Berger closed the Book, bowed his head, and led the group in a simple prayer of thanks for the day's blessings and a plea for the night's protection, Cassie's mind was awhirl with the words she had heard.

Cry unto the Lord. What a thought! But it was a thought that had never occurred to her. All her tears, all her pain, had been inward. No ear heard, no voice answered, no one shared the silent anguish. Did He?

With murmured "Good nights," Cassie crept into her wagon and the nest she had made. There, alone again (or was she?), looking up at the dark sky (or was it?), she wept her tears and dared to hope they were seen; she cried out her heartache and loneliness and dared to believe they were heard.

7

MEREDITH WIPED HER LIPS DAINTILY, FOLDED HER serviette, and placed it on the table. It was whisked away almost immediately.

"Mummy's washing today," Emmie explained, adding, "she couldn't do it yesterday, of course, because we were getting ready for comp'ny." And she disappeared in the direction of the lean-to kitchen.

I'm the "comp'ny," I suppose, Meredith thought a little uncomfortably.

From the kitchen she could hear energetic sounds of clattering and banging. Elva, she imagined, was dipping water from the range's reservoir into a tub or boiler.

Waking from her night's sleep, the first good one she had had in several days, Meredith had been dismayed to realize there were no facilities for her morning bath. While she was pondering this dilemma, Emmie had tapped on the door and entered, carefully bearing a water pitcher. Made of heavy tin, its inexpensive origin was somewhat disguised by the prettily painted flowers that embellished it.

"Good morning, Aunt Meredith," the small girl said primly. Then, in a burst of confidence, she added, "I know you're not my aunt, but I can't go around saying 'cousin,' can I? Anyway, it's prob'ly 'cousin twice removed' or something like that, so Mummy says I may just call you 'Aunt,' unless you object."

Emmie, not waiting for an answer, was settling the pitcher beside its matching basin on the small washstand, her tongue between her lips in serious concentration.

"It would help," Meredith said kindly, "if you didn't watch the water while you walk."

"It would? Oh, thank you! I'm usually quite a spiller. Of course, I'm only nine, and this is very heavy."

"You did very well."

Emmie opened a compartment in the washstand, removed a snowy towel, and hung it on the towel rack. From a drawer she produced a small soap dish containing a bar of soap.

"Buttermilk glycerin," Emmie said proudly, and Meredith had an idea its match would not be found in the soap dish at the communal washstand just inside the kitchen door.

"It's absolutely pure," the child explained, "and has no alkali or any injur—injur-i-ous substances." And Meredith had an idea this was a direct quote from the catalog's description.

"Five cents a cake," Emmie continued naively, "and we kept it just for you." She rubbed the treasured extravagance with her fingertip, put the finger to her nose, and inhaled blissfully.

"We've eaten, Aunt Meredith, but Mummy says not to hurry. You can have breakfast when you're ready."

And Emmie tripped happily away, her face rosy with the importance of her responsibilities.

As the child's worn boots clattered down the carpetless stairs, Meredith turned to her trunk and its bulging contents. One after another she held up and then laid aside the garments she had packed, some of them new for the trip, and now all seeming out of place. Being "in style" was certainly out of style here in the backwoods.

Every dress or suit she owned had a tight-waisted skirt, spread at the ankle to a width of four or five feet and often

lined throughout with rustling taffeta (Why was it so important to rustle? she wondered now). Sleeves, tight from wrist
to elbow, burgeoned into huge puffs at the upper arm and
shoulder—and all horribly crushed, Meredith noted with
dismay. Would Cousin Elva be amenable to ironing them?

With an uneasy feeling that washday, already delayed
because of her arrival, might not be a good time to broach
the subject (but—bright thought—didn't ironing day immediately follow washday?), Meredith finally chose a skirt
of shepherd's plaid in black and white, faced halfway up
with canvas and velvet-piped, lined, of course, with
rustling taffeta.

Her dimity shirtwaist, with white linen turn-down de-
tachable collar and turn-back cuffs, double-pointed back
yoke, gathered front and back, and featuring puff-top
sleeves, was the simplest item she owned. Purchased with
the offices of Brandt Brothers Textiles in mind, she had
hoped it would lend itself graciously to country living.

Country living! Meredith glanced from the window at
the parsonage yard, obviously a farmyard, for it seemed
the Victors kept chickens and turkeys and cows and horses. Beyond its environs ran the road that was the main
thoroughfare of Wildrose. Even as she watched, a buggy
passed. The occupants, two middle-aged ladies, looking
very much alike and dressed in what was undoubtedly
gingham (with not a puff and probably not a rustle between them) waved and called a greeting to Emmie, who
was now struggling across the yard with a pail of water.

Poor Emmie—she seems fated to go through life as a
bearer of water, Meredith thought wryly.

Emmie, apparently happy for an excuse to rest, set the
pail down, waved, and shrilled, "Good morning, Miss
Dovie! Good morning, Miss Dulcie!"

And the "Double Ds," as Meredith promptly dubbed
them, were soon lost to sight behind the bush that bounded each road and field and yard.

Meredith finished her grooming and descended the narrow stairs, puff sleeves and canvas-stiffened skirt touching the walls on each side. Already beaded with perspiration but with a warm smile for her husband's cousin, Elva Victor came from the kitchen, brushing a strand of fair hair back from her sticky forehead.

"Coffee or tea?" she asked, offering the morning's choices. "And how do you like your egg?"

"Coffee, please. And soft-boiled on the egg." It never occurred to Meredith to offer to help.

Seating herself at the round oak table in the dining area of the house's main room, Meredith studied the "parsonage." Last night, more tired than she could ever remember being, it had been lost in the gloom of the kerosene lamp. Now, awaiting her breakfast, she studied it critically; it would be "home," but for how long?

Home was built of logs squared and set together as tightly as possible; the remaining space between had been chinked. Windows were narrow and high. The floor was made of wide boards.

Nevertheless, the irregular walls were whitewashed, the windows covered by stiffly starched lace curtains, and several bright rag rugs had been placed strategically over the board floor.

At the other end of the room there appeared to be an Axminster rug of floral design, fringed on each end. And clustered around it was an overstuffed parlor suit in crushed plush, consisting of a sofa, rocker, and two parlor chairs, all heavily tufted and ornamented with fringe and tassel valances.

In a corner gleamed a fine hardwood piano with carved panels and trusses. On its "music desk" stood an open hymnal, and its lid was covered with a felt scarf with an embroidered six-inch drop.

At the side of one of the chairs a basket contained sewing, and several items of color and beauty were displayed on the buffet: an engraved Tilting water set with cup and slop, a silver-plated biscuit jar, a crumb set with fancy handles and beaded border, a porcelain clock, and a dinner castor with five ruby bottles.

The simple, even rustic home was enhanced by these items that first-cousin-once-removed Gerald and his wife, Elva, had brought with them from their former life. Meredith approved. There was no need to live like bumpkins even though you lived among them, she muttered, with a more-than-fleeting thought of the man Dickson Gray and his part in her embarrassment and chagrin. Considering herself a model of competency and efficiency, Meredith's self-image had been challenged. And following as it did on her ultimatum to Emerson, she had come out fighting.

"Here, Auntie—here's your coffee."

In Emmie's small hand the delicate cup joggled in its saucer.

"I forgot not to look at it," Emmie said guiltily, spilling only a little as she set Meredith's morning coffee on the table.

"I'm sure you'll get onto it," Meredith encouraged. "You see, my dear, you can do anything you set your mind to. Learn that now, and it will stand you in good stead all your life."

"Yes, Aunt Meredith," responded the small girl and made her escape.

Tapping the egg in its little cup and carefully removing the top shell, Meredith added salt and pepper and considered Emmie's well-worn and much-faded dress, the neatly patched tablecloth, and recalled the frayed collar and cuffs of her cousin's shirt, revealed without particularly close inspection. Life in the bush pastorate, it appeared, was one of sacrifice.

Meredith's memories of Gerald were vague. She had been a small child when he had been a young man already fired with the zeal of a missionary and preparing to do great things for the Kingdom. His passion had embraced a life of deprivation in Timbuktu, if that was required of him; his commitment and obedience had led him to this remote corner of Canada's bush. Elva, as dedicated as her husband, had gladly left family and comfort for the uncertain provision of this new work in the backwoods.

Meredith, however, had come for a far different reason. Rather than coming *to* something, she was running *from* something: Emerson Brandt's betrayal and, yes, his lack of confidence in her as a woman of ability.

Adding cream—so thick it plopped from the pitcher— to her coffee and stirring it absently, Meredith found her thoughts going back to the betrayal. In the three years of her service to Brandt Bros., Meredith had risen to a place of responsibility in her department, called Product Control. And when the position of head of the department came open, she had every reason to hope she might be selected.

Along the way, Meredith had attracted the attention of Mr. Emerson Brandt. Son of the chief executive and already an important part of the business, Emerson was considered a catch by all the girls in the office. But he had turned his attention on Meredith Deane.

It had been a sort of passionless relationship, she supposed, thinking back. Emerson's affections were primarily directed toward the business. But so were Meredith's. Heart and soul, she gave herself to the concept of equality.

For it was true that fields of industry and of intellectual interest were being opened to women; educational opportunities were possible, and the success of girls' colleges and "annexes" was unquestionable. Coeducational education, however, where young men and women met on terms of absolute equality, still met with vigorous opposition, unfortunately.

In the industrial and work area, new fields were constantly opening, and it had gradually come to be accepted that the true limit to a woman's activity should be determined by her powers and abilities rather than by the arbitrary rulings of custom and prejudice.

Feeling secure in her capabilities and having earned a place of some responsibility and limited authority, Meredith had felt confident her name would be considered for the vacated department headship.

Over dinner one evening in one of London's finest hotels, Emerson had, casually but surely, destroyed her dreams. "Of course," he had said, taking a sip of water as they awaited their soup, "Magnus Greene will be taking over now that George Miller is retiring."

Meredith, likewise engaged in sipping water, had started so abruptly that her water slopped. With the perfect aplomb that marked Emerson's life, he dabbed at the offending damp spot with his serviette. "I shall request the waiter not to fill the goblets so full" was his disapproving comment.

"Emerson, wasn't I considered?" Meredith knew her voice held a touch of anguish. The disappointment had been so keen and, really, unexpected.

"It's generally felt, my dear, that a man is more adroit —that is, basically better qualified for responsibility."

Dazed, Meredith had restrained herself from a wild "Bosh!" Emerson would be shocked at the lack of propriety; Meredith breathed deeply a few times and said, "Well, what do you see for me, then, in the future? I have certain ambitions, Emerson." Her distress threatened to sweep her into incoherence.

"Why, my dear, I should think marriage is the ultimate achievement."

"I'm surprised," Meredith couldn't keep from saying, "you find me *adroit* enough to manage your home!"

Emerson's handsome face had borne a gentle smile as he reached his large white hand across the table to clasp hers. "Well, my dear," he had said indulgently, "not quite yet, of course. It's something you can work on."

"Work on?"

"Our home will be one of some position in the city. Running it will be a challenge to you. I'm sure."

"A challenge, Emerson? What's so challenging about running a house, I'd like to know."

"My dear, my dear," Emerson's voice was soothing, "keep calm. Remember—you've never done any housekeeping. It's a very great responsibility, I assure you."

"Child's play!"

"You've lived all your life with domestic help, Meredith," Emerson had reminded her. "And while we'd start off with someone to help with the heavy cleaning, perhaps, and the gardening, the great burden of it would fall on you. It will take great skill and resourcefulness and—and organizational ability."

"Any simpleton can keep house, Emerson! I'm an educated woman, a trained woman—" She had almost added "a woman of discipline" but thought better of it in the face of her present lack of control.

"And it will take all of it," Emerson had assured her, "to be a wife and mother."

For a moment they had sat and stared at each other—Meredith hostile, Emerson the picture of rationality.

Drawing a deep breath, Meredith had asked, "Are those my options? Go back to the office as I was, or run your household?"

"Oh, come now—"

It was at that point that Meredith—slowly, deliberately, head high, eyes blazing—had removed Emerson's ring from her finger and laid it on the table between them.

It was then Emerson—dispassionately—had picked it up and put it into his pocket.

* * *

The slam of the screen door startled Meredith from her thoughts.

"Mum! Mum!" It was small Buddy, Emmie's little

brother. "I've found ol' Biddy's nest! It's in a corner of the empty manger, and she's settin' on a whole bunch of eggs."

Meredith picked up her cold coffee and stepped into the kitchen, where Buddy danced in excitement around the washtub.

"There—," Elva said automatically, indicating the slop pail, and Meredith, with a grimace of distaste, poured the remainder of her coffee in with last night's potato peelings and goodness-knew-what-else.

"It got cold on me," she said apologetically. "Is there more?"

Drying her hands, Elva Victor picked up the coffeepot, shook it, found it empty, and dumped the grounds in the slops.

"I'll make more," she said.

Meredith never knew she drank tea for lunch because she finished the coffee supply with her second and third breakfast cups.

Weak, she thought. Careful measuring would take care of that.

8

DULCIE AND DOVIE SNODGRASS, BOUNCING along in their buggy, went over their already well-rehearsed plans.

"Am I supposed to ask him, Sister, or will you do it?"

"I'll do it, Dulcie. After all, I'm the experienced one. Dear Terence won't mind if I use my expertise on someone else. After all, it's for a good purpose."

Dulcie wasn't quite as convinced as her twin. "I'm very nervous about this, Sister. You'll have to be very circumspect about it. Think how dear Mama would feel if you were too forward."

"Mama could look over my shoulder, Sister, and would find no fault in how I'll go about it. One must be bold and still be reserved, titillate without—"

Dulcie's eyes widened, and her hand flew to cover her mouth as it fell open.

Noting her sister's obvious dismay over her use of the word, Dovie added, "It's not as bad as it sounds, Sister. One may titillate—or, if you insist, arouse interest without teasing. Oh, it will take some cleverness, but I feel I'm up to it."

"I certainly hope so," Dulcie said doubtfully. Having put their hands to the plow, so to speak, there was no turning back.

"Pull up, Sister!" Dulcie said sharply. "Someone seems to be in some sort of trouble."

A dusty, tarpaulin-covered wagon was drawn into the shade at the side of the road just ahead of them.

"Oxen! Fancy that! No one around here uses them anymore."

Dovie passed the strange rig cautiously. With a swift glance at her sister, she pulled her horse to a halt.

"Do you see what I see, Sister?"

"It's—it's a girl. I think."

The oxen stood, heads down, only occasionally nibbling at the tall grasses at their feet. On the wagon seat a figure slumped—a figure in a man's coat. But the hair spilling over the collar was brown and curling, and the face, when it turned in their direction, was young—young and incredibly weary.

"Go back, Sister, and see if something is wrong."

Dulcie bounced from the buggy and tripped back until she stood alongside the wagon. The face that looked down at her was white, the eyes anxious.

"Hello there!" Dulcie piped. "Can I help in some way?"

"I—I think I must be lost," the girl said.

"Well, where are you going?"

"Prince Albert. I'm going to Prince Albert."

"You're way off the proper road," Dulcie said sympathetically.

Dismay filled the big, thick-lashed eyes. The girl seemed to clutch at her midriff; perhaps she was pulling the coat more securely around her.

"Are you all right?" Dulcie asked kindly.

"I have to get to Prince Albert," the girl repeated.

"Well," Dulcie said with a sigh, "you need to take the next road to the left and keep going straight until you come to one much more traveled than this one. It's several miles from here. You've strayed quite a bit off course. You're surely not traveling alone." Dulcie's glance flicked to the body of the wagon and the probability someone was in it, under the canvas cover.

"How long will it take me to get to Prince Albert?" the girl asked.

"You won't make it today—that's for sure."

The small figure drooped.

"Tell you what. You wait here until my sister and I get our business done at the next farm, and on our way back you can follow us home. We'll be happy to have you stay with us overnight, or as long as you need to rest up a bit."

"I have to get there."

"You'll make it in better shape if you take an extra day or so. Now just do as I say—you get your rig turned around, and before you know it, we'll be back."

About to leave, Dulcie added, "I'm Dulcie Snodgrass, and that's my sister. What did you say your name was, dearie?"

"Cassie—Cassie Quinn," the girl answered dully.

"Well, Cassie, I'll see you in a little bit." And Dulcie turned reluctant steps toward Dovie and the buggy.

"Maybe we should turn around and go back," Dulcie said when she had explained the situation to Dovie.

"She's lived in that rig for some time—I can tell you that," Dovie said knowingly, casting a final glance back at the worn wagon and even-more-worn oxen. "But we're on a mission, Sister. Don't you feel sort of a *dedication* about this?"

"I'm trying, Sister. I just hope Anna appreciates it."

"She will, Sister—you'll see. Love is the very finest emotion in the world, I'm sure."

"I didn't know we were expecting it to be a love match."

"Sister!" Dovie cried reproachfully. "We can't look at this simply as a matter of convenience!"

"But I thought that was the whole idea—"

Dovie sighed. "It's plain to see you've never been in love. Love is *vital*, Dulcie! We can't cold-bloodedly commit our sister to a loveless relationship. That's what makes this whole idea so exciting. Now don't look so worried. Just settle back and watch an experienced woman at work!"

"I hope you're more experienced at love than you are at driving, Sister," Dulcie said grimly, holding on for dear life as Dovie urged the mare to a swift trot at the same time she tried to maneuver the buggy through the narrow gate onto Digby Ivey's land. Tilting dangerously, they straightened out and sped on toward the buildings.

Digby Ivey had been one of the fortunate ones who arrived with funds enough to set himself up in style. His barns were adequate, his fields fenced, his house made of lumber rather than logs.

Digby himself came from the shadow of the barn door, striding toward the buggy, a strong, well-built man of 50, his hair—on both face and beard—vigorous, his teeth white and strong. Watching him with new eyes, the sisters gained a fresh appreciation for their choice.

"Well, Sister," Dovie said in a swift aside as Digby approached the buggy, "we surely can't have too much trouble falling in love with him."

"Anna, you mean."

"Anna, of course."

"Miss Dovie! Miss Dulcie! Nice to see you. Will you get down and come into the house?"

"Not today, Mr. Ivey," Dovie answered. "Maybe next time."

"Next time," Dulcie echoed.

"What can I do for you then?"

"Well, you see, it's like this, Mr. Ivey. One of our plow horses has a shoe that's loose. It's more of a job than we can cope with, although Anna is a wonderful worker—do you know Anna very well, Mr. Ivey?"

"Not well, I'm afraid. I knew your father, of course."

"Dear Papa! He would be so proud, the way Anna is coping. There's no one to equal her, we always say—don't we, Sister?"

Thus appealed to, Dulcie chimed in, "Oh, absolutely! You'd go a long way and look a lot farther to find anyone as capable as our Anna!"

"But the loose shoe is just too much."

"Not because she couldn't do it if she set her mind to it, Mr. Ivey! Oh, no indeed! But she is a woman, Mr. Ivey, and Sister and I feel we need to protect her from er—herself. She's a wonderful homemaker too. In fact, this loaf of bread is of her own baking; we know she would like for you to have it."

Dulcie produced the sacked bread and thrust it into the arms of the surprised man.

"Why, thank you," he managed. "And please thank Anna for me."

"Oh, we will—we will!"

"And the loose shoe?" Dovie prompted.

"I'll be glad to do it for Miss Anna. How about day after tomorrow? Can it wait that long?"

"Perfect! Make it afternoon, Mr. Ivey. If I know Anna, she'll have fresh scones ready about teatime. The workman is worthy of his hire, you know!"

And with this sally, the twins made their departure.

If they had cared to look back, they might have seen Digby Ivey sniffing the fresh bread appreciatively and his son, Shaver, coming from the shadows of the barn.

They might have seen his eyes light up at that rare blessing, bread, actually *anything* baked by hands other than his own.

* * *

The despairing gaze of Cassie Quinn watched the buggy and its occupants until they were out of sight, lost in the never-ending bush.

What a relief it had been when the wagons traded the never-ending prairie for the bush! One full day they had moved into it, mile after mile, watching the first scattered growth thicken until eventually it surrounded them. Feeling that at long last the end of the arduous journey was in sight, Cassie had felt the tears on her cheek.

A few more long days, a few more camps. Regularly falling behind the others during the day, Cassie always pressed on until each evening found her camping with her fellow travelers. And now, finally, Prince Albert was within a day's journey.

This morning, with the wagons barely out of sight, Cassie felt the first discomfort. Shifting her position on the hard seat, she had waited for it to pass. Eventually she had left the wagon and walked beside the oxen. Even then the misery continued and increased until she mounted the wagon again and, gritting her teeth, endured the stabbing pains.

It was at least two months too soon for the arrival of the baby. Concern for her condition turned to anxiety when physical symptoms further indicated a problem.

At first, urging the oxen to an increasing speed, she had hoped to overtake the others. Finally, knowing this was hopeless, Cassie had submitted her pain-racked body to the jolting wagon and prayed.

Every night the weary travelers had gathered at the campfire for Bible reading and prayer. And every night Cassie, wondering at it all, had crept into her bed—to study the silent stars and try, tentatively, to pray.

The phrase of the first night's devotions, "desired haven," was a concept that had fixed itself in her mind. How very badly she needed a refuge! With the comfort of Rob's arms denied her, she felt more than ever adrift in the green sea that had swallowed her up. And how she longed for—greatly desired—a sanctuary. Would God have such a place for her and for Rob's baby—or was it all a dream, as distant and unreachable as the stars?

Now, riding out the pain and the fear, Cassie found herself crying out the most heartfelt prayer of her young life: "O God! If You're out there—bring me to my desired haven!"

＊ ＊ ＊

Dulcie and Dovie, spanking along at a brisk pace on their return trip from the Ivey homestead, could soon see the empty road; nowhere was there a glimpse of the travel-weary wagon and its similarly abused occupant.

"I was afraid of that," Dulcie lamented. "She kept saying she had to get to Prince Albert. Well, she won't make it today—that's for sure."

"Looks like she turned in the right direction," Dovie said, studying the tracks. "If she doesn't get lost again she'll hit the main road by nightfall."

"You should have seen her up close, Sister. She was tuckered out, maybe sick. Her eyes, big anyway, were simply huge in her pale little face. She looked so small and frail under that big coat she had clutched around her. If we could have kept her a day or two and fed her up—"

"She won't find anyone on that road," Dovie said with a nod in the direction the girl had taken. "The MacTavishes are gone; won't be back for a couple weeks."

The sisters clucked to their horse and continued their trip home.

"How do you think it went, Sister?" asked Dovie.

"I don't know," Dulcie said somewhat doubtfully. "Seems like you could have got the ball to rolling a little bit more than you did."

"We can't scare the man off, Sister! I accomplished what I wanted. He'll be over day after tomorrow. And we've got work to do!"

Dovie urged the horse to a smart clip. They eventually pulled into their own barnyard. Then each to her special task—Dulcie to put the mare away and Dovie to locate a screwdriver, seek out one of the plow horses, spend a few minutes getting its heavy foot raised, and a few longer minutes prying and digging under the edge of its shoe until it could definitely be said to be loose.

PLACING THE PRETTY LITTLE EGGCUP INSIDE HER empty coffee cup, setting it onto her plate, and adding her knife, fork, and spoon, Meredith rose from the table, picked up the neat stack of her breakfast things, and turned toward the kitchen.

The small room was crowded with wash day's necessities. Elva was bent over a tub set on a box or base of some sort, laboriously pulling sopping items from the soapy water and scrubbing them vigorously on a washboard. Scrub, swish down into the water, scrub again, swish, eventually decide it's clean, hold it to the attached wringer with one hand, turning the rollers with the other hand—that seemed to be the system. From the wringer the clothes fell into another tub to be rinsed, and the swishing-and-wringing routine was repeated.

Working her way past the operation, Meredith looked for a place to set her dishes. On the table was a bowl of something white and thick.

I hope that's not lunch! She considered the possibility with a slight shudder and was relieved when Elva gathered up the cuffs and collars of a white shirt and thrust them into the "goo," wrung them out, and dropped the shirt into a basket of similarly treated garments.

"Just put them in the dishpan," Elva suggested, glancing up from her task and noting the dishes in Meredith's hands. Meredith put the soiled dishes into the pan on the back of the stove.

"Now where's an empty pan for the bluing?" Elva muttered, studying the heaped chair, piled floor, and steaming boiler. "I think one's here somewhere! There never seem to be enough pans or enough hands," she said cheerfully.

"If the dishes were done first," Meredith said thoughtfully, "that pan would be empty and available when needed."

"Of course!" Elva agreed, never mentioning the late-breakfaster's just-added contribution. "I'll have them out of there in a jiffy!"

And the busy little woman thrust her already-red hands into the dishpan and speedily finished the washing-up process.

"Here," she said, smiling, and handed Meredith a dish towel. The surprised guest obediently wiped the dishes, looked around for a place to put them, and, at Elva's nod, found the proper shelves.

While Elva emptied the dishwater and made bluing of small balls of compressed powder tied in a piece of white cloth, adding the solution to the last rinse of white clothes, Meredith studied the kitchen cabinet's arrangement.

"It seems to me," she murmured, "the fruit dishes should be put toward the back—I'm sure they're used less often than the eggcups, which are probably used every morning. And the cups—"

Meredith spent 10 minutes evaluating the cupboard situation and arranging into carefully planned areas the dishes, mostly battered, in her cousin's cupboard. Stepping back and studying the result with satisfaction, Meredith thought scornfully of Emerson's opinion of her housekeeping abilities. Just let him take a look at this!

Feeling rather self-righteous, Meredith noted the pile of just-washed white garments and, lifting them one by one, immersed them helpfully in the white substance she had identified as starch.

Behind her, Elva's eyes widened in dismay as Meredith's fingers dipped Emmie's summer-weight gauze vest into the stiffener, followed by Gerald's best "Pure Lisle Thread Underwear," a relic of better days and saved for Sunday wear. Imagining her husband's acute discomfort when standing—starch-encased—to preach turned Elva cold. Gerald's fine lawn handkerchiefs followed . . .

Fortunately, at that moment Gerald's voice called through the kitchen's steam and clutter, and both women turned to him gladly. Noting his wife's stricken face, the minister took in the washday drama. Removing the milky, emulsion-saturated items from his cousin's possession, he chided, "Now, Meredith, try and be content with acting like company, at least for today."

"Why don't you take Meredith with you this morning?" Elva suggested quickly. "It can't be much fun to watch me doing the laundry. Or she might like to go for a walk with the children."

"Oh, yes—let's take Auntie Meredith for a walk!" pleaded Emmie, and her mother, with resignation, took the basket of clothes the girl had been tugging toward the door and the clothesline.

"Do you like washday, Auntie Meredith?" Emmie asked when the trio were trudging down the sun-bright road. "*I* don't like it," she went on, not waiting for an answer. "'Course, I don't have to help when school's on. It's very hard work, isn't it? And it spoils a perf'ly good day."

"Perhaps you could make a game out of it," Meredith suggested. "Perhaps you could sing a little song and work in rhythm to it. Like 'Here we go looby loo, here we go looby li; soon all the dirt is gone, soon all the clothes are dry!'"

"P'raps," Emmie said doubtfully while Buddy began cackling, "Loopy, loopy, loopy," and kicking up dust until Meredith's skirt was coated and she wished she had never invented the little melody. The gritty problem wasn't helped when a horse and rig approached, drew alongside, and came to a stop, with Meredith and the children standing in the tall grasses to the side of the road.

"Uncle Dickson!" the children chorused, while Meredith fumed to herself, Is everyone in the entire territory related to them?

"Where's Jennie, Uncle Dickson?"

"She's home helping Gran."

"But washday was yesterday!" (Did everyone in the entire territory wash clothes on Monday?)

"Yes, and that makes today—"

"Ironing day! But our mummy is *washing* today—"

"What a terrible mistake!" "Uncle" Dickson said in a shocked tone. "The whole week will be upset! Does that mean you won't be mending tomorrow? What will happen when Saturday comes and you've got more work than you've got week?"

Emmie giggled, and Buddy worked up a veritable froth of dust in his hilarity.

"I shall help her, of course," Meredith said coldly. "We shall both iron *and* mend tomorrow."

Dickson Gray's speculative gaze seemed to take in the fashion plate before him, from the crown of her carefully piled auburn hair to her special glove grain button shoes, promised by London's finest emporium to be oil-tanned for wet weather, half double-soled, with worked button holes, pegged and warranted, and now as dusty as the draggled hem of her skirt, so carefully chosen that morning for country living.

"Our irons weigh five-and-a-half pounds—Daddy says that's why they're called sad irons," Emmie explained. "Jennie's too little—"

"Little as she is," the man answered, turning his attention to the child, "she can help Granny in several ways. She was standing on a chair ironing serviettes when I left."

"She doesn't know how to mend, Uncle Dickson," Emmie said wisely. "P'raps she can play tomorrow."

"Perhaps. Now—I'm going to Bailey's to borrow a piece of equipment I need. Anyone want to ride with me?"

"Me!" "I do!" shrieked the children, who began clambering up behind the buggy's one seat to stand side by side, clutching the biscuit-patterned leather cushion tightly.

Holding her skirt aside with one hand, Meredith reached for the strong brown hand held out to her and stepped lightly up beside Dickson Gray.

"We like to ride with Uncle Dickson!" Buddy shrilled into her ear. "Show Auntie Meredith how fast Slicker can go!"

"Slicker?" Meredith questioned with raised eyebrows.

"City Slicker," Dickson Gray explained, adding, "hold tight now!" And with a slight loosening of the reins, the beautiful bay responded, his long legs lifting high, his neck arched, obviously eager to perform.

"City Slicker," Meredith said brightly, holding to the armrest. "And I suppose you're Country Boy."

"That's the idea," Dickson Gray said lightly.

"Uncle Dickson brought Slicker with him from the coast," Buddy breathed into the tangle of Meredith's escaping hair.

"Well, that accounts for the 'City Slicker' part; what about the 'Country Boy' angle?" Meredith asked. "A description, no doubt!"

"But not an apology," Dickson said. "A statement, I like to think."

"Uncle Dickson is really the city slicker," Emmie explained, leaning her face between the two adults. "He only came because Jennie's mummy died, and he wanted his granny to help look after her. Isn't that right, Uncle Dickson?"

The man's jaw had tightened as the child talked, but his tone was gentle when he said, "That's right, honey."

"So you really are a city man?" Meredith asked.

"No!" Dickson's answer was firm. "I've only been here about five years, but it's a lifelong commitment for me and for my child. I guess you could say I'm a transplant and I've taken root in the bush."

Meredith was thoughtful, wanting to know more but not feeling free to pry. Fortunately, the children could be counted on to have little or no inhibitions.

"You see, Grandpa Gray died and Granny couldn't carry on alone. Daddy says she needed Uncle Dickson as much as he needed her. Right, Uncle Dickson?"

"Right, Emmie."

"Only now Granny is getting all stove up with rheumatiz!"

Dickson Gray smiled at the child's frank explanation of his grandmother's physical problem.

"And," Meredith concluded, "that's why the illustrious Miss Janowitz—"

"Janoski."

"Whoever—was coming. To help with the household responsibilities and no doubt with Jennie's care."

"That's right. And by not coming"—Dickson Gray's dark face was grim—"she's dumped a very big problem on me." The man's eyes, deep-set under heavy brows and separated by a strong nose, were brown shot with shafts of light in the bright sunshine.

"Poor Granny's fingers are getting all curled up—she can't hardly milk at all!" Emmie piped over their shoulders. "And Jennie's too little, isn't she, Uncle Dickson? Isn't she too small?"

"Yes, I'm afraid so."

"Daddy said it was praying time. We've been praying, haven't we, Buddy? Have you been praying, Uncle Dickson?"

"Sure have. When I wrote Miss Janoski I exhausted the only lead I had. It's a busy time here in the bush—summer's work is endless—and for the life of me I can't think of anyone who'd be free to help, at least to the extent we need it."

"O ye of little faith," quoted Meredith, as though inspired.

"Do you think so?" The man turned the sun-lit blaze of his eyes on her. "I think I'm looking at it realistically."

"Ye have not, because ye ask not," Meredith said, almost completely depleting her store of Scripture.

The dark brows drew together as the man thought about what Meredith had said.

"If this is some kind of levity, Miss Deane—"

"Yeah, if this is some kind of levity—what's levity, Uncle Dickson?" Emma chirped.

"It means excessive or unseemly frivolity," Meredith began.

"What's friv—"

"And, sir," Meredith lifted her chin as she spoke to the man now engaged in controlling a fractious horse, "you may believe me to be serious! Why would I joke about such a thing?"

"Miss Deane," Dickson Gray said elaborately, "I'm afraid I have no idea what you're talking about. We were discussing, I believe, my grandmother's physical condition and my need to obtain the services of a housekeeper. Now would you pick it up again from there?"

"And I, Mr. Gray," Meredith responded, just as elaborately, "am offering to do the job for you."

"You, Miss Deane?" There was unbelief in the dark-hued gaze when it turned on her and studied her face.

"Do you have some objection, sir?"

"Not at all. Just let me lay out the situation to you—Gran can't do anything anymore—Jennie is five years old. This is a full-time, backbreaking, dawn-to-dark job. It will take grit, good health, patience, and considerable understanding of the running of a farm home."

Shades of Emerson Brandt! Meredith thought with a burst of impatience.

"I've had complete charge of a corps of office work-

ers—I guess I know a little about competence, Mr. Gray,"
she managed.

"But running a house—"

"Any simpleton can run a house, Mr. Deane. It's simply a matter of organization and priorities."

"Well, if you're sure." She read the doubt in his eyes.

"I'll start Friday."

"Cleaning day!" piped Emmie.

10

NEVER HAD THE OXEN WALKED SO DELIBERATELY; it seemed to Cassie they must stop if they slowed any further. Never had the wagon jolted so sharply; each jar passed through her hurting body as though she were an extension of the wagon itself.

In spite of the bright sunshine, Cassie shivered inside the tent of the big black jacket she had drawn around herself not only for warmth but also for comfort. In the fog of her pain and despair she imagined it was Rob himself, loving her, encouraging her, holding her.

In fact, it became easier and easier to believe it *was* Rob. For surely someone other than herself was driving; she held the reins in listless hands, and they eventually slipped out of her nerveless grasp completely. Still the oxen rambled on.

Cassie had turned the wagon in the direction the two ladies had indicated; the Prince Albert road lay ahead, they had said. The oxen would find it . . .

Where she had strayed from the proper road she didn't know. Her last logical thinking had been in a small hamlet—Meridian, she thought. Sympathetic folks there had said, "Yes, the wagon train passed two or three hours ago, heading for Prince Albert," and "No, you really can't miss them if you keep straight on down this road."

The swaying of the wagon and the endless thud, thud of the heavy feet of the oxen had drifted her into her first dream state. "Rob," she had said, "you didn't tell me about the bush. I feel like an ant creeping in monstrous grass. As far as I can see there's nothing but grass, grass, and big, big sky."

But it wasn't grass. It was miles and miles of poplar and birch and she-didn't-know-what-all. And it was all tangled together with bushes, some of them thick with blossoms, a few bearing small berries. The ripe ones she knew as saskatoons; she had promised Rob a saskatoon pie.

"How can I find our place in all this, this secretive bush?" she questioned the silent Rob. "Where is my desired haven?"

Dreaming, talking, perhaps praying, she had lost all sense of time and place—until the oxen had finally stopped and had begun cropping grass, having taken a wrong turn somewhere along the way.

"Straight down this road," the kind lady had said.

Once again it was thud, thud, and creak, creak. Wrapping her arms about herself inside the jacket, Cassie slipped into a pain-filled forgetfulness.

When the yoke of oxen wandered, the thrusting growth at the side of the road turned them back. Finally, in their perambulations, the wagon jounced over a broken tree limb. Cassie, swaying and unaware, slipped from the wagon seat to the heaps of gear that were piled around and beneath her.

Tumbled into a hollow and half-hidden by the stretching tarpaulin, rocking hypnotically by the seesawing motion of the rig, Cassie slept.

When a break in the greenery presented itself, the oxen with one accord turned into it. A gate ajar would have indicated to a thinking creature that humanity passed this way; for the dumb creatures, some unknown impulse turned their heavy feet, and the wagon creaked along a trail more dim than they had known.

Even their weary eyes recognized the signs of human habitation. With a final groan, the wagon stopped beside a well, and the animals lowered thirsty muzzles into a trough—an empty trough.

With the patience that had made them invaluable to Rob and Cassie, the oxen dropped their heads and closed their eyes, and eventually only an occasional twitch of their hides indicated they were any more alive than the silent sleeper in the wagon bed.

* * *

Whether it was a real meadowlark that woke her or a part of her dream, Cassie didn't know. But she woke to silence—no meadowlark, no voices, no creaking wagon. No creaking wagon!

With a start Cassie came fully awake. Coming to her knees, she raised her head above the edge of the wagon. Where was she?

It took only a minute to study the well and the empty trough; the log barn, closed and barred; the shed; what she supposed was a granary; an empty hen house.

And, finally, the snug log house.

Silence reigned. There was no welcoming bark of a dog, no busy cackle of a hen. Stillness reigned. No barn door swung in the slight breeze, no clothes danced on the line, no smoke lifted from the stovepipe.

Into the silence and the stillness, piercing sharp and clear and sweet, a meadowlark!

Her Angelus—hers and Rob's. A siren song, luring them ever on. A beacon, as though from a lighthouse beckoning through a sea of grass to a safe harbor—a snug haven.

A haven.

With a sense of the perfect rightness of it, Cassie swung herself over the edge of the wagon, to the ground. With a strength hardly her own she turned to the well, dropped the bucket, waited for it to fill, and hauled the water to the surface. The thirsty oxen drank deeply; Cassie dipped her face into the last pailful and drank, finding the water sweet and satisfying.

Stepping to the oxen's heads, she grasped the harness and urged them forward until they stood in the barnyard. In the midst of unhitching them, she stopped, embraced the thick necks, and whispered her thanks: "You blessed beasts!"

The bar to the heavy door lifted easily enough, and Cassie lugged the harness inside, draping it over the empty stalls.

A gate at the side of the barn led into what she assumed was a meadow: unplowed, unsown, green with native grasses—and empty. Into this she turned the oxen and closed the gate on their lumbering forms.

"Go ahead," she urged. "Eat and rest."

The slumbering misery in her body gripped her savagely. With a whimper, Cassie leaned on the fence rail. With the easing of the cramp, she turned toward the wagon to prepare it, like the oxen, for its enforced rest, however long that might be.

The brightness of the day dimmed suddenly, and, glancing up, Cassie could see the dark clouds gathering, ominous and heavy. The quiet atmosphere took on new meaning: a storm was brewing.

Even as she looked, lightning split the heavens, followed closely by a drumroll of thunder. Its echoes had not faded before Cassie was pulling certain personal items from the wagon and what limited supplies of food remained.

The first heavy drops were splattering the canvas as she struggled to shove the remaining goods into a pile well away from the open ends, where rain was already slashing inward.

"Rob," she murmured, hardly knowing she spoke aloud, "it got me here."

The treated canvas, guaranteed to have no tar in its "composition" and "entirely free from anything calculated to crack or burn," had staunchly resisted "rot or mildew from damp," and not broken from being "too hard." Throughout, it had protected her possessions and made a home for her and Rob. Now she watched the rain mark it with runnels as the dust of the trail ran down onto a Saskatchewan homestead. Whose homestead, she didn't know.

Staggering under her load and her pain, Cassie stumbled toward the cabin—house, for it was larger than a homesteader's first shelter. Low, glistening white in the rain, the windows winked at her in what she felt was a friendly fashion.

For a moment her heart failed her—the door was locked! But realizing the improbability of this, Cassie leaned on it, and the heavy boards, dry under a wide overhang, swung open.

Knowing in her heart it was empty, still Cassie paused, wet and weaving in her sickness and weariness, and called aloud: "Hello! Hello! Is anyone home?" For she knew immediately it was a home, not just a house.

The door had led directly into the lean-to kitchen. Queen of all it surveyed, a handsome range gleamed black and silver along one wall. A massive kitchen cabinet, supplies bulging behind glass doors, a first-grade kitchen table with flour bins, drawers and slides, and tin-covered, copper-bottomed pots and pans, all spoke of a well-cared-for and perhaps much-loved home. To Cassie, it seemed to reach caring arms for her.

Dropping her gear onto the linoleum, its bright pattern only slightly dimmed by dust, Cassie made her way toward the attached room. Here, obviously, the family lived. A large table dominated one end of the space; here too a thin layer of dust hid the sheen of its polished surface. Bulked around a shining heater, an old-fashioned sofa and several comfortable chairs suggested conversation and relaxation. Books and magazines dominated the living area; pictures and touches of crystal and silver spoke of someone's delight in the beautiful, even the rare.

Crossing the room, Cassie pulled open a door and found what she was looking for—a bed. Summoning her strength, Cassie pulled back the beautiful hand-crocheted white spread and revealed snowy sheets of bleached cotton.

Sagging and staggering, Cassie removed her outer garments, managed to untie and remove her boots and worn stockings, turned to the bed's luxury, and, as though sinking onto a mother's bosom, laid her tired head and hurting body down with a sigh of contentment. Just before all sight and sound faded away, she pulled from the foot of the bed a woolly red blanket, drew it over her shaking form, tucked her head down into its folds, and lost herself in its comfort.

Overhead the thunder rolled; rain thrummed on the heavily shingled roof and ran in silver torrents down the windows. Wrapped in a borrowed blanket in a strange bed and buried in the secret silences of the bush, Cassie slept—slept and dreamed that she had come home.

11

CLOSING THE SCREEN DOOR BEHIND HER, ANNA filled her lungs with the sharp morning air and thanked God for Wildrose.

Older than her sisters when they had made the life-changing move from England to the Northwest Territories, Anna had borne an adult's load along with their parents, and her memories of the trying days differed from those of her sisters. Her memories were filled with an overwhelming sense of awe that they had survived, and even thrived. God had been good, a veritable "stronghold in the day of trouble," and the Snodgrass family had been among those hardy souls who endured.

Explorers and fur traders had paved the way. The influx of settlers had started slowly, but by the middle of the century the prairie was dotted with settlements, and the pace quickened until the invasion carved endless trails across the trackless plains.

To facilitate, heavy flat-bottomed York boats had navigated a river seldom more than 12 feet deep and often less. At times they were hauled by crews of laboring, sweating, singing men. At times they were propelled by sweeps so long and heavy that the boatman had to rise to his feet with each pull and sit down to complete the swing.

An even stranger "craft" was seen and heard crawling across the prairies: the ungreased Red River cart with its piercing creak-crawk. Made entirely of wood, pegged or bound with rawhide, a balanced plank platform with an affixed railing was mounted on the axle. The result was a conveyance that was light and strong but which could carry a ton of weight. With wheels removed, it floated like a raft. Needing no lubrication, its squeal accompanied many a family over stretching, din-filled miles.

As often as not, hundreds of rabbit skins stitched together covered the lumbering carts rather than canvas. The trains of carts endured such hardships as blizzards and sub-zero weather, quagmires, thievery of its animals, sickness, and deprivation of every kind.

The Snodgrasses had been spared the torment and torture of travel by Red River cart, choosing the easier river route. Mama, horrified by the endlessness and emptiness of the prairies after her beloved England's greenery, had insisted they press on to the bush country. Reaching The Forks, as the meeting place of waters was called, the Saskatchewan's south branch flowed on to become the main watercourse for the prairies, and the North Saskatchewan flowed through forest and parkland.

And here Mama's satisfaction had been boundless. Stepping on land, she had ordered, "Set up the tent, Charles—we'll go no farther." And in the trees they rested. Mama's tent had moved eventually to the area now known as Wildrose, to be replaced soon by a shack and later a small, tight cabin.

Now, at Anna's back a substantial house, log, of course, was home. Mama's few treasures had been unpacked; Mama had experimented with their good hard grain, adjusting her English recipes until satisfied they were just like those her sisters were enjoying in faraway England.

Even now Mama's scones were baking in the morning's first oven, to be reheated in the afternoon when Anna's many tasks would make it difficult to stop and bake. Teatime often featured other treats, such as a toasted muffin, thin slices of bread, or, in season, cucumber sandwiches.

But today Dovie had insisted on "Anna's scones."

"They're not my scones," Anna had insisted, "any more than they're your scones. After all, you know how to make them too. And it would be a great help if one of you would make them today; I'll be greasing the farm machinery and—"

"Greasing machinery!" Dovie squeaked.

"And today, of all days!" Dulcie continued.

"Why not, for goodness' sake?"

"Well—um—er—isn't this the afternoon Digby Ivey is coming to fix Barney's shoe?"

"So?"

"Sister and I feel we should show him the courtesy of tea. I'm sure Mama would have done so!"

Invoking Mama's name was heavy artillery indeed.

"It's the decent thing to do, Anna!" Dovie cried. "And we must be appropriately dressed. Greasy clothes won't do it!"

"You girls take care of tea today. Just call me when it's ready, like always," Anna instructed, "and I'll wash up, like always."

The twins looked at each other in desperation. All their cajoling and arguing hadn't changed Anna's position, although she had finally capitulated and agreed to make the scones, baking them early in the day so that she could get on with her work.

Dovie and Dulcie made one more attempt: "We did decide, did we not, Sister, that we are going to see if Digby might be interested in getting in the crop?"

"The crop that poor dear Papa put in," Dulcie said as she wiped her eyes of their ready tears, "never knowing he wouldn't harvest it."

"Digby must be talked to, all right," Anna agreed, and only partly understood why her sisters turned away with relieved faces.

Yes, Anna concluded now as she so often had, Wildrose was indeed their land of promise. For them, and for great numbers of sturdy Hungarians, Russians, Ukrainians, and Magyars, the land-hungry from England and Scotland, from eastern Canada and the United States, even for a few immigrants from China and India, this was their place.

Whole communities spoke French or one of the Scandinavian tongues; there were Doukhobors and Mennonites, remission men and rogues, bachelors without number, and family men. Many knew little or nothing about farming; finding themselves unsuited for farm life, they helped start villages or went on to established towns.

The weak caved in, those who were morally or physically unable to cope with the sawflies, dust, drought, mosquitoes, grasshoppers, early frosts, the prairie fires. The strong stayed; women, half-demented by isolation, cut notches in doorframes and window frames to keep track of the passing of days too lonely to endure. They buried their babies, one after another; sometimes they buried their husbands, married again, and carried on.

And so had begun what came to be known as one of the greatest migrations in history—and the last to a new frontier. Eventually the terrible trip would become a memory as the first tough years passed; the soddy or the shack of poles and tarpaper became a more substantial home. And always, everywhere, through it all, neighbor reached out to neighbor.

And they still did, for the migration, if anything, was gaining momentum; thousands upon thousands of land-seekers continued to pour into the vast area that was there for those eager enough to take it and stubborn enough to hold it.

Just yesterday Anna had watched a lone wagon, oxen-drawn, plod past. The hunched figure on the wagon seat typified the indomitable spirit of the west, and Anna's heart had lifted in a salute.

The Snodgrasses had endured thus far; it was up to her, Anna felt, to carry on. And with God's help, she would do it.

She would take it upon herself to talk to Digby Ivey about helping with their work.

❊ ❊ ❊

Dovie lifted soapy hands from the pan of dishwater, and Dulcie, wiping away at a breakfast mug, turned with her as though by a single thought, to peer out the window at Anna.

"Do you think she's onto us, Sister?" Dulcie asked anxiously, her gaze fixed on the figure of her older sister, dallying in a way most unlike her, apparently gazing thoughtfully at the greening wheat field.

"How could she be? We haven't done anything yet," Dovie responded. "But I've got plans."

"What are you hatching up, Dovie?"

"It's that dreadful gown she's wearing! We've got to get her out of it before Digby comes, and into something pretty."

"How do you plan to do it, Sister?"

"You'll see."

"Anna's no numbskull, Sister. You'll have to be very clever not to arouse her suspicions."

"Trust me, Dulcie! I'm experienced at this sort of thing, after all."

Dulcie looked doubtful. "As I remember it, you didn't do much courting with Terence, Dovie. You walked out together a few times—and it was all a very long time ago. I don't know that *modern* people have time for all that socializing and kissing of hands."

"Women haven't changed," Dovie said firmly, "nor men either. Flirting comes natural to us—and men just naturally respond. Now go get the mending basket while I go get Anna's second-best dress."

"The mending basket?"

"It's mending day, isn't it?" Dovie said a trifle impatiently.

Dulcie watched unbelievingly as Dovie took the scissors and carefully snipped the threads to the hem of the skirt. By now an expert at loosening horseshoes and hems, Dovie finished the job in what she called "jig time."

"Sister! What are you doing?" Dulcie's tone was sharp.

"I can't mend if it isn't torn, can I?" Dovie asked practically.

"But why does it have to be torn?"

"So I can have an excuse for hanging it out here with the other mended items."

"I confess," Dulcie sighed, throwing up her plump hands, "I don't understand what's going on!"

"Anna is going to have to change dresses—quickly," Dovie answered, threading a needle expertly.

"Why can't you just have it hanging here, without going through all this rigmarole?"

"But, Sister," Dovie said severely, "that would be dishonest, wouldn't it—having the dress hanging with mended items when it hasn't been mended?"

Dulcie was stunned into silence by her twin's devious thought process. Finally, she managed, "I didn't know you were such a—a humbug, Sister!"

"All's fair in love and war," Dovie responded blithely. "Now get to work on the linens. Mama's best tablecloth has worn through."

12 ✿

WITH A BREAKFAST OF OATMEAL AND TOAST
over and Elva engaged in cleaning up the kitchen,
rinsing the beans that had soaked all night—adding fresh
water, an onion, and a ham hock—and putting them on the
back of the range to simmer all day, and with Gerald off to
the seclusion of his "study," Meredith settled down at the
dining room table to write a letter to Uncle Homer and
Aunt Marie.

It is with pleasure I take pen in hand to write you,
dear Uncle and Aunt. After a most trying trip, about
which I shall be silent, I have arrived in Wildrose,
which is truly the back of beyond! I must admit that
Elva and Gerald seem to have retained something of
their former way of life. Others, I'm sorry to say [as
she wrote, Meredith thought of Dickson Gray], are inclined to be boorish.

Buddy, who is six, and who owned only a home-
made bat and handstitched leather ball, welcomed the
manufactured ones I unpacked from my trunk. Emmie, nine, a dear but quaint little thing, might have
shown more enthusiasm for the gift I brought her—a
toy set of sad irons. But I daresay she'll have fun with
them when her little friends come to play.

Gerald was delighted with his book, *The Open Secret*, by Hannah Whitall Smith (a good suggestion on
your part, Uncle!), while Elva professed herself over-

whelmed by the white china silk parasol. (Noting the atrocious, plain, tan-colored cotton hose she wears, I rather wish I'd brought a good grade of those ribbed lisle hose the girls in the office wore. I may even find myself pressed by sympathy into sharing with her a pair of my own silk plait hose, trusting I may order more if needed.)

Except for a few walks, I haven't been beyond our home environs (it's early yet, of course). That is to say, we haven't had any social occasions. Numerous parishioners have stopped by, often to leave butter or eggs or a piece of fresh-slaughtered meat, and all seem friendly, although terribly bucolic! Church on Sunday (held in the schoolhouse) should be an interesting exposure to the district, probably on its best behavior!

As for Wildrose and the area in general, words truly fail me. It is most beautiful in its greenery. It even smells good! But one must come to grips with a sensation of being wrapped in bush. I, for one, need not feel claustrophobic, because I realize my time here is of my own choosing.

I haven't begun to identify the local flora and fauna, except to gather a few handfuls of a berry called 'saskatoon' (which you may know as Juneberry or serviceberry), which cousin Elva made into a pie (much too mild, and it would have been improved with a dash of lemon, although, when I gently suggested it, Gerald laughingly asked where it would come from. He said I might as well ask for a banana—which, by the way, neither Buddy nor Emmie has ever tasted or *seen!*).

There is a plethora of birds here! The country seems almost alive with ducks and partridges; Gerald says they are as thick as "sandhill fleas." "Whatever are they?" I said, and Gerald pointed out a few red marks that I have been scratching!

Fields are overrun with gophers; the children get

a bounty for them, but Buddy doesn't have very good success at trapping (or pouring water down the gopher hole, which is his method!). Emmie can't abide the idea of collecting gopher tails but says she is very good at knocking down crows' nests! Coyotes abound, and I shudder at night at their yapping. Deer are scarce now, and bears are seen only occasionally. Thank goodness!

I think I shall need to have something to do to keep myself busy. You know me—just a workaday girl! And so I have made a decision to assist one of Gerald's parishioners—a widower with a small girl. Don't be alarmed, dear Aunt! Decency and decorum prevail here (and everywhere that good Queen Victoria's influence reaches!). There is a grandmother in residence, but she is incapacitated. I understand I shall be a sort of housekeeper-cum-nurse. It should be rather amusing, but hardly a challenge. I still look forward to my return to the professional world of business and trade, where I may find challenges worthy of a woman's intelligence and capabilities.

I've run on far too long, dear Uncle and Aunt. You have fond thoughts from

Your loving niece,
Meredith

P.S. I see I've used an abundance of exclamation marks. But that's the kind of place this is!

As Meredith was addressing an envelope, enclosing her letter, and sealing the envelope, Elva bustled in from the kitchen.

"How about a fresh cup of tea?" she asked.

At Meredith's agreement, Elva soon produced the brew and a plate of warm toast with a small pot of raspberry jam.

"I believe I could get a taste for your bread, Cousin," Meredith complimented. "And it makes delicious toast."

"Yours will be just as good, I'm sure," Elva commented.

Meredith paused with her cup halfway to her lips and said, with some surprise, "I hadn't thought of that. I suppose I will be doing the baking."

"Saturday."

"Baking day?"

Elva laughed. "Don't be intimidated by schedule, Meredith. It's really sort of a myth, at least in my household. Too many things come along to ruin any such plans —a call I need to make with Gerald, missionary meeting, a trip to Meridian for supplies."

"I see great advantage in a schedule," Meredith said. "I do like to be methodical and businesslike."

"It does give a feeling of accomplishment at the end of each day," Elva said. "Of course it can work in reverse too; if you don't get everything done you had planned on, or if things go awry, you soon feel you are falling dreadfully behind."

"I'm a great one for system, having an inventory of every facet—what must be done, the equipment necessary, the time allotted, the final effectiveness."

And drawing a blank sheet of paper toward her, Meredith added brightly, "Like this, for instance." And with pen poised, she added, "The bread recipe if you please, Elva."

Now it was Elva's turn to be surprised. "You mean you don't know how to bake bread?"

"Well, of course I know—measure, stir, mix, and so on. I just don't know the ingredients." Meredith was slightly impatient with the delay.

"Cousin," Elva asked slowly, "just how much experience have you had in the kitchen?"

"I've made candy," Meredith answered.

"Candy!"

"Fudge—taffy. And to do it I followed a recipe! Now, if you please—the bread recipe."

"Wheat bread or white bread?"

Meredith looked blank. "Wouldn't the recipe be the same?"

"You might want molasses in the brown bread."

"Well—white bread."

"Potato bread?"

"Potatoes? Why would I want potatoes in bread? No, no—plain white bread."

"From starter or yeast?"

Noting what began to look like dismay in Meredith's eyes, Elva went on kindly: "We'll assume Granny Gray has yeast cakes on hand. Now, will you want to make one loaf, or perhaps four, or six? It will make a difference in the amount of ingredients," she added hastily, watching Meredith's face.

"Six loaves?" Meredith said weakly.

"It's probably on the table for every meal. And I don't think you want to do this more than once a week. It could—er—throw you off on your schedule for, say, cleaning day."

"Four loaves," Meredith said faintly.

"That's probably a good guess; if you miss it," Elva said comfortingly, "you can fill in with biscuits."

Meredith drew another piece of paper forward. "The recipe for biscuits, Elva—"

"Soda or baking powder?"

* * *

"She's a pure babe in the woods, Gerald!" Elva confided to her husband.

"A babe in the bush, more like," Gerald said with a shake of his gray-touched head. "She has no idea what life is like here. Thank goodness Dickson Gray's place is far from crude. In fact, it's quite comfortable for a homestead —much like the Jameson place since Abbie and Jamie joined their efforts. The Grays were among the first people here, years ago. Grandpa Gray had all the hard work done before Dickson took over. Now take people like the Redekops."

"Just barely out of the dugout they lived in for the first 10 months. Even the children have it hard in homes like theirs."

"In more than one home in the district," the caring pastor said, "children are hard at work before they're eight years old—milking, planting, the girls ironing."

"And baking. You know, Gerald, little Jennie will know more about what needs to be done than Meredith!"

"Could be a big help. Or—could be embarrassing!"

"I'll make it a point to drop in as often as possible."

"That's my girl!" said Gerald recalling the almost overwhelming situation that had faced Elva, a city girl, when they arrived on the frontier. Her gallant and graceful adjustment was one he would not forget, and his few words paid her only a small portion of the accolade she deserved.

My part, the pastor thought, turning toward his books, is actually much easier. Aloud he said, "You women—in the bush—you are the ones to make the sacrifices and pay the costs."

Elva, giving her tan-colored cotton stockings a hike, turned to Friday, and cleaning day, with a swelling heart.

"Come, Emmie," she called up the stairs, "time to get the kerosene and go over the mattresses for bedbugs!"

13

IT WAS THE CALL OF A BIRD THAT WOKE CASSIE from a sleep so heavy it might have been drugged. But it was not a meadowlark.

And neither was there blue sky above her. Rather than the smell of axle grease, her nostrils filled with the faint scent of well-laundered bedding.

Momentarily bewildered, Cassie lay still, her eyes moving to the low ceiling, the whitewashed walls, and finally the curtain-covered window through which a bright sun was casting lace-shaped shadows on a snowy counterpane.

The sound that had awakened her came again—cocky and clear: a rooster.

With a gasp, Cassie thrust herself up onto her elbows. Once again all was quiet. In a flood of remembering, it all came back: the pain and her fear, the plodding oxen providing a hypnotic lullaby, their wandering from the proper trail . . .

And the snug house, appearing before her like a vision in a fog-bound dream. Now, as then, there was no indication of a human presence. But there were chickens.

Swinging her feet over the side of the bed, Cassie paused, placing her hand cautiously on the swelling that was Robin. She released her breath in a great sigh when she felt movement—and no pain.

"Thank God!" she whispered to that distant Deity. Was it possible He was nearer than she knew?

Making her way silently over scattered rugs to the

doorway, Cassie studied the larger area—the living room she remembered from her study of it the day before. And again, it seemed a place of refuge.

"Surely love lives here," was her dim awareness.

On the sideboard were several photographs. Cassie stepped to the side of the lovely oak piece and, one by one, picked up and studied the pictures of her absent hosts.

Most of them were of two people—a young man (though just how young Cassie couldn't assume) and a woman. Age was indistinct. But he was handsome and she was lovely—a striking pair.

Stepping to the window, Cassie pulled back the curtain to study the couple more closely. His was a rugged build; his smile was close to being a laugh, with his head thrown back and his teeth strong and white. She was exceptionally feminine—almost dainty; her smile was sweet, her eyes soft.

Gently, Cassie replaced the pictures. On a small table a large Bible caught her attention. Turning the pages, she could see many passages were underlined.

Curious about the names of the people she assumed were the homeowners, Cassie turned to the front of the Bible. Sure enough, inscribed in a flowing hand was a name: Moira MacTavish.

Moira—what a musical sound!—as musical as "meadowlark," Cassie thought. Was it possible it might be as significant?

At the side of the Bible lay a stack of letters, addressed to Mrs. Moira MacTavish. And, near the bottom, one for Andrew MacTavish. Andrew—and Moira.

As Cassie moved around the room, additional proofs of the occupants' names appeared on magazines and papers, and recorded on the flyleaves of many of the books that dominated the room.

Andrew and Moira MacTavish—obviously as Scottish as they sounded, for many of the return addresses on the mailed material were Edinburgh, Scotland. Additional mail bore an Ontario address; no doubt there were relatives and friends there also. A great percentage of homesteaders were from Ontario, having settled there earlier and eventually moving on to the beckoning West.

Again the rooster's crow broke the morning stillness. Cassie started, wrenched from reverie. Passing through the lean-to kitchen, she stepped outside. Light blazed from a cloudless sky; now she could hear rustlings from the bush that surrounded the farmyard's clearing. Birds were tuning for morning rhapsodies, and wings flashed in and out of the greenery.

Into the yard she had previously thought empty straggled a mother hen followed by a bevy of chicks. From the direction of the outbuildings the rooster lifted his greeting to the day one more time.

What a lovely spot! Cassie thought. How peaceful, how—homey!

The wagon, weather-beaten and weary, seemed to doze where she had left it. Of the oxen, turned into the meadow, there was no sight.

Crossing the yard, scattering chickens as she went, Cassie opened the gate and slipped into the grassy pastureland. With the sun warming her shoulders and the dewy grasses cooling her bare feet, she walked across the fragrant area. Noting a few tiny strawberries, she stooped from time to time to pick one, savoring the sweetness and realizing how hungry she was—ravenous, in fact.

Cresting a small rise she found not only her oxen but also two cows, one obviously ready to calve and the other with a newborn calf, and a team of horses grouped around a small slough. At her approach a score or more of ducks rose with a great splashing and beating of wings.

"Nesting," was Cassie's observation, as some darted from the reeds and rushed to open water before lifting off.

With a great burst of gladness Cassie flung her arms

around Bib, so named because of the apronlike brown coloring down the throat and across the breast. Suddenly the dumb ox was dear to her.

"Naturally, the other one has to be named Tucker," Rob had decided. To Cassie they had remained "those creatures," or simply "the animals."

Now, heart full of gratitude, she hugged the long-suffering pair, and they bore it, as all else, stolidly.

The calf, head down, tail up, eyes liquid, and legs spraddled, was having its breakfast.

"Hey, leave some for me!" Cassie pulled the reluctant baby away, knelt in the wet grass, and, turning the teat toward herself, pulled and squeezed. The milk from the bulging bag shot forth readily, splattering Cassie's face before she directed its warm stream into her thirsty mouth. Her laugh, her first laugh, spilled across the meadow, raising a catbird from the grasses and turning the horses' heads in her direction.

"It's all yours," she said to the impatient calf dancing awkwardly around the mother, and it went back to its interrupted meal.

But there's plenty for me, she thought with satisfaction as she rose from her knees and walked back toward the house. Next time, I'll bring a pail. Or perhaps the cows come to the barn by habit each evening. Depends on how long they've been alone here.

That they were alone and untended was clear. But the cattle and horses had plenty of pasture and water, and the chickens, probably running free even before their owners left the premises, could survive by scratching and pecking the abounding insects and wild seeds.

Now, almost as though she were the pied piper, a mother cat and her kittens fell into step behind her. Sleek and obviously doing well on the bush's abundance of mice, the tabby curled herself around Cassie's legs, and her babies tumbled over one another in eager pursuit.

"And there's plenty for you too, my dears," Cassie assured them, kneeling again and stroking first one and then another. They certainly weren't wild, another indication that their owners had not been gone unreasonably long.

And an indication that they would be back.

"I'll face that when it happens," Cassie thought, strangely at peace, and dug a sack of oatmeal from her supplies in the wagon.

For Cassie, a farm-raised girl, chopping kindling was no problem. From the ample woodpile she carried what she needed to start a fire in the range and keep it going for the day's meals; from the well she lifted a pail of cold, sparkling water.

Opening cupboards, she was to find all she needed in the way of a pan for the oatmeal, utensils for stirring and eating, and a pot for her tea.

While the oatmeal simmered, Cassie took a clean pail, turned upside down on the back porch, and, with it swinging in her hand, made her way again to the meadow and the cow. As she had suspected, there was plenty for her—and the cats.

"Good girl!" she offered in appreciation, patting the obliging cow before she turned back.

Bit by bit, Cassie moved needed items from the wagon into the house—a bit of sugar for her oatmeal, tea for the home's big brown pot, a scrap of hard brown soap to wash her dishes.

Locating a snowy dish towel in a kitchen drawer, Cassie promised the absent Moira that she would handle all the MacTavish things carefully and leave them in as fine a shape as she found them.

Drying her bowl, spoon, cup, and the cooking items, Cassie found herself humming a portion of a hymn her companions had used to close each nightly devotion time on the trail. Pregnant, alone, and lost, Cassie raised a thin, sweet note of praise from the hidden, secretive recesses of the bush—"Praise God, from whom all blessings flow," and felt herself not alone after all.

While the oven was hot, Cassie mixed up a batch of biscuits and baked them. Two of these, with a little jam, were her lunch. And more milk, of course.

In the drowsy heat of the afternoon Cassie rested, not rousing until the cow's bawl issued from the fence by the barn. Again she milked, feeding the cats and straining the rest and putting a panful in the cellar to keep cool. In a day or so she would have enough cream to skim and make butter. Her mouth watered at the prospect.

As the day faded to a long twilight, Cassie lit a lamp that had been filled with kerosene. The wick had been trimmed, and the chimney shined. Setting the lamp on a small table at her elbow, she seated herself in a comfortable rocking chair and opened the Bible—Moira's Bible.

"Perhaps I can find my verse" was the thought that prompted her.

Never had Cassie gotten away from the scripture that had spoken to her heart that first night on the trail when, alone and frightened, she had sought her wagon bed without Rob's arms to comfort her. It was something about a storm, the man had read—and about crying out to the Lord—and about coming at last into a desired haven.

Cassie only knew it was from the Book of Psalms. She found Psalms readily enough; the Bible opened to it automatically, particularly one section.

Here, on a page well-thumbed by the absent Moira, Cassie supposed, was something the reader had found meaningful. Cassie's eyes were drawn to an underlined portion: "He that dwelleth in the secret place of the most High shall abide under the shadow of the Almighty. I will say of the Lord, He is my refuge and my fortress: my God; in him will I trust."

With indrawn breath Cassie read it—again and yet again. The haven! Was this it?

"The secret place—the shadow of the Almighty—my refuge and my fortress"—were not those havens?

Had Moira MacTavish needed the haven? And had she found it?

Cassie read and reread the scripture until she knew it by heart. Then she continued her search for "her" scripture.

Finally, disappointed, she put the Bible away. Tomorrow she would begin a systematic reading of Psalms and keep on until she found and learned for herself God's promise of a desired haven.

14

DOVIE TUCKED A STRAY CURL INTO PLACE, smoothed her hands over the skirt of her prettily flower-sprigged dress, and looked anxiously out the window.

"Anna's somewhere the other side of the shed," Dulcie reported.

"And she's in that greasy denim smock!"

"I don't know, Dovie, how we're ever going to get her cooperation."

"Well then, Sister, we'll just have to boldly do it for her! Here—tuck this back hair in for me, will you? I look absolutely too helter-skelter with it all falling down."

Dulcie worked on her twin's hairdo until they heard the rattle of Digby Ivey's buggy. Glancing in the mirror over the washstand by the back door and pinching her already-rosy cheeks to add to their freshness, Dovie opened the door and sailed outside, Dulcie at her heels.

"Mr. Ivey!" they chorused in glad welcome.

For a large man, Digby Ivey stepped down from his buggy with a light step. His broad, bearded face was split by a genial smile. The sisters exchanged approving glances.

"Well, here I am, as promised. Now where's that loose shoe?"

"In the barn, Mr. Ivey," Dovie said graciously and led the way, shoulder to shoulder in a companionable manner (although her shoulder was much lower than his).

Dulcie, following, thought they made a fine pair. The trick was, however, to substitute Anna for Dovie.

In the barn the sisters produced the tools needed from their father's supply and stood back as Digby Ivey went to work.

"All that hair, Sister! It makes me shiver!" Dulcie whispered.

"It's the sign of a very masculine man, Sister. Poor, dear Terence was cultivating side whiskers when I saw him last—"

"Terence was a boy compared to this—male creature, Sister!" Dulcie quavered. "I trust Anna can cope with all that masculinity."

"He'll do just fine!" Dovie insisted. "See how capable he is!" Dovie watched as the big hands wrestled the old shoe from the gelding's hoof. "He's what's called a fine figure of a man. That's got to be a size-34 waist, Sister, and a 35-inch inseam."

Dovie's speculations were based on orders made for "dear papa" with his 40-inch waist and 34-inch legs. She had helped choose Papa's heavy blue denims with "large bib apron and shoulder straps; cut full size, with double-lock stitch seams warranted never to rip," the "indestructible buttons, front and hip pocket and rule pocket and felled seams." Even now several pairs, in various stages of wear, were awaiting the day when another man, pear-shaped like Papa, might be found and given the overalls.

Now studying the bent figure, Dovie realized he was clad in "Cow Boys' Saddle King Overalls"! Even in the barn's dim light she could tell they were "extra-heavy nine-ounce brown duck; two front, one hip and one watch pocket; double seat and made double all the way down inside of legs; double-lock stitched seams; riveted buttons and—"

Dulcie, always in tune with her sister, quoted in an exultant whisper, "'Words cannot express their goodness.

The world has never produced their equal!' Do you realize what this means, Sister?"

"It means he's wearing his second-best clothes!"

"And that he's come—courting! Oh, Sister!"

Silenced by the magnitude of their discovery, the sisters clutched each other in an ecstasy of joy over the encouraging sign that Digby, himself, had designs on Anna.

Anna!

"Dulcie!" Dovie whispered urgently, "you keep him here another 10 minutes and then see that he comes in the house for tea!"

Dulcie looked rebellious at the instructions, but Dovie shook her arm fiercely and gritted, "He's dressed for tea, Sister! And I've got to have time to get Anna cleaned up! Now do as I say!"

Leaving a nervous Dulcie behind, Dovie trotted at full steam to where Anna was smearing the binder with noxious grease.

"Time for tea, Sister," Dovie reminded brightly. "You know the tradition!"

Anna laid the grease aside reluctantly, wiped her hands on a rag, and then turned toward the house. Dovie hurried inside to pour the boiling water into the teapot, to heat it prior to steeping the brew itself. Anna, at the washstand, scrubbed her face and hands. Then, face ashine, hair damp, and hands red, she toweled briskly.

"I'll just slip on a clean apron," she decided. "That way I can go right back to the job."

At that moment Dovie turned abruptly from the stove, a full pan of warm, clabbered milk in her hands. Her about-face occurred just as Anna was about to pass.

"OH! EEEE!" shrieked Dovie, as the brimming pan and Anna collided.

Anna gasped, then stepped back and surveyed and smelled the bodice of her workaday smock, dripping with slimy sour milk.

Before Anna could recover herself, Dovie snatched Anna's second-best dress from the array of mended items waiting to be put away, thrust it in her sister's hands, and said, breathlessly, "Quick, Anna! Go change before Dulcie and Digby come in and see you looking such a mess!"

Anna, outmaneuvered, went to change.

Dovie, cheeks scarlet, eyes sparkling, heart aflutter, met Digby and Dulcie at the door.

"Come right on in, Mr. Ivey!"

"I'll just wash first," Digby said, and Dovie thrust a fresh towel into his hands as he turned to the washbasin. In an aside to Dulcie, Dovie gave a massive wink, all her dimples dancing around her pink little mouth.

"Now, Dulcie," Dovie said, bustling from stove to worktable, "the scones are in the warming oven, and everything else is on the tea table. If you'll just make the tea—oh, come on into the other room, Mr. Ivey. As you may know, it's our custom to stop for tea every afternoon. Anna carries on so ably in dear Mama's absence.

"Oh, there you are, Anna! My, don't you look nice? You'd never know she was just out there servicing the machinery, would you, Mr. Ivey? Anna carries on so ably in dear Papa's absence."

Mr. Ivey seemed hypnotized by a splatter of something white in Anna's hair. To distract him, Dovie prattled on, "Now these scones—" as Dulcie bore down upon them with the napkin-covered tray "are another indication of Anna's abilities."

"Let's just begin, shall we, Dovie?" Anna suggested gently, and Dovie subsided. But not without a nudge in Dulcie's side and a significant nod in Digby Ivey's direction.

"Er, Mr. Ivey, do you take sugar in your tea? Milk?"

As the affable Mr. Ivey was being served, Dulcie and Dovie hovered over him, anticipating his every need.

"We miss dear Papa so much," Dovie said, and Dulcie's eyes moistened. "I must say it's good and natural to have a man sit up to tea with us again."

"Any time!" the agreeable man replied, and the twins exchanged glances.

"I'm sure you miss your father a great deal, having lost him so recently," Digby Ivey continued. "I think I mentioned it at the time of the funeral—but then, so did many other neighbors—that I'd be happy to help in any way I can, at any time. Please don't hesitate to call on me. If I can't come, Shaver will."

"Thank you—God bless you—that's so kind of you," the Snodgrass sisters responded.

"The fact of the matter is—," Dovie began.

"I think Anna had something she wanted to talk to you about," Dulcie continued.

Digby Ivey turned bright blue eyes on Anna.

"Not just now, I think, Mr. Ivey," Anna said thoughtfully. "Another time, when we're not at tea, perhaps."

"Of course," the man concurred, "that might be better. If it's of a business nature, Miss Anna, drop in when you're driving by on your way to Meridian, or give me a holler when I'm passing."

When the pot had been drained and conversation depleted, Digby Ivey, with grace, thanked the ladies, said his good-byes, and left. But not before a solicitous Dovie had wrapped the remaining scones in a paper bag and pressed them on the departing man—"A reminder of Anna's baking skills."

Flushed with success, Dovie and Dulcie gathered up the tea things.

On her way to her room to change her clothes, Anna paused and turned to her sisters.

"Girls," she said, "you're overdoing it." The "girls" looked thunderstruck and dismayed. "I don't think we need to work so hard to get Digby to take on the work here," Anna continued. "You were rather, well, obvious about it. I'll speak to him in a more normal situation, and I'm confident he'll agree to help us. But no more buttering him up, all right?"

Frozen momentarily into immobility with the tea things in their hands, Dovie and Dulcie began to breathe again, heaving great sighs of relief. Anna hadn't suspected a thing!

"Personally," Dovie whispered to her sister, "I thought it went very well. Did you count how many scones he ate, Sister?"

And, thoroughly unchastened, the twins crept away to come up with more plans in the plot to woo Digby Ivey.

15 🌸

A S DICKSON GRAY AND COUSIN GERALD STRUG-
gled and strained to cart her belongings down the
narrow parsonage stairs, Meredith couldn't help but remember the dismay in Dickson's black eyes when he had
first spotted her mound of baggage at the train station.

"Do you think, Meredith, you should leave some of it
here?" Elva was saying. "Some of those things, you said,
are winter items; perhaps you'll be back here before then."

"I plan to carry through with my commitment," Meredith said firmly.

Elva looked doubtful, even concerned. "It's a very
heavy commitment, I'm afraid. Are you sure you know
what you're getting into?"

"I'm young, strong, and healthy. I have a certain
amount of brains—enough, I'm sure, to cope with household responsibilities. And," Meredith said as she tapped
her roomy Boston shopping bag, "I have my recipes!"

"Bread and biscuits." Unmentioned were dumplings,
johnnycake, pastry, gravy, salad dressing, soup, preserves,
meringue, mincemeat, sauerkraut, catsup.

Not considered were the poultices (mustard, carrot,
cranberry), the syrups (rhubarb, garlic, fruit), the oint-
ments (sulphur, belladonna).

Did cousin Meredith know that onions, cooked as a
sauce and eaten freely, were considered a cure for constipa-
tion—or that pumpkin seeds, peeled and beaten in with

sugar until a paste is formed, are a recognized remedy for worms? Was she aware that kerosene, as well as providing light, played an important part in family health care, properly mixed and dosed—for quinsy, colds, toothaches, croup, bunions, corns, and scalp care?

Did she know how to fix creaking bedsteads? Did she know that pepper mixed with camphor gum and put at the edge of a carpet would keep out moths? Did she know lamp chimneys could be toughened against breaking by immersing them in cold water to which salt has been added? Did she know the entire length of a new wick should be dampened with kerosene so it would light? Would she eliminate onion odors by setting a container of vinegar on the stove and letting it boil?

Would she wash certain colored garments without soap, using water in which pared potatoes had been boiled, to prevent the running of colors? Would she remove wagon grease from clothes by rubbing the spot with lard? Would she bleach white items by spreading them on the grass in the sun?

Did she know to save the downy part of feathers? Would the ashes from her range be flung down the openings in the toilet? Would she put a small potato on the spout of the kerosene can to keep the kerosene from spilling?

Elva's poor head was spinning at the remembrance of just a few of the things she had needed to learn—and was still learning. Wisdom kept her from mentioning them.

So it was with a blithe smile and a buoyant spirit that Meredith made the trip to the Gray homestead. Old Mrs. Gray, who immediately invited the new member of the household to call her "Gran," welcomed her warmly. Bent with age and years of work, twisted with rheumatism, Gran had, with small Jennie's help, managed a simple supper.

Without being told, the child helped clear the table and, standing on a stool, washed the dishes while Meredith dried. Meredith had a chance to observe where the dishpans were kept and the soap and dish towels. Putting the dried dishes away, she studied the cupboard's arrangement, acquainting herself with equipment and supplies. Different from many bush homes, this one had, besides a cellar under the kitchen floor, a pantry. With its tidy collection of household goods and foods, this seemed a great boon to Meredith.

Before she retired for the night to the small upstairs bedroom allotted to her, she located the pots and pans, brought eggs from the cellar, checked the bread box (low—much in need of tomorrow's replenishing), the oatmeal, the eggcups (too far back in the cupboard), and felt a sense of smug satisfaction in her adroitness where housekeeping was concerned. Each day, each task, she felt, would go equally well with following precise instructions, and with due regard for "product control" here, as in her office days.

A little uncertain about her responsibilities to Jennie, Meredith was relieved when Dickson took the child by the hand and headed off for her bedroom. First, however, Jennie kissed her grandmother and looked uncertainly at Meredith.

"Good night, Miss Deane," she finally said, politely.

"'Meredith,' dear. And why not 'Aunt Meredith,' if that's the custom?"

"Come, Miss Deane—Meredith—," invited the eldest member of the household, "sit down and rest a bit. Tomorrow will be hectic enough."

"Hectic? I truly trust not," Meredith said brightly. "I suppose there's some baking that needs to be done."

"I'm afraid so. I haven't been able to pummel dough for a long time. We've struggled along with Dickson doing the kneading. I'll be so grateful to have him relieved of some of the load. And Jennie, little as she is, can help. She can help you locate things, and she knows the routine pretty well.

"Dickson, you know, moved here so that I could help him raise his daughter. He had been running the family transportation business on the coast but turned it back to his father in order to move here and take up the homestead when Dick, my husband, died."

Eager to reminisce about happy times, Gran explained how her husband had been part of the mad scramble for gold along the Fraser River, the fame of which had spread like wildfire until there were 4,000 miners, it was said, in a stretch of seven miles.

"And did he strike it rich?" Meredith asked politely.

"Not hunting gold," Gran said, "but he did find a way to make a good living. The cost of freight, you see, was enormous—50 dollars just to get a pair of shoes delivered. Dick started a freight line, which later expanded into what we called a transportation enterprise; our son Dickens took over, and then Dickson became a part of it."

"And he left it to bring Jennie to you when his wife passed away," Meredith said.

"And we've gotten along famously too—until this wretched rheumatism crept up on me!" Gran flexed her fingers painfully. "And that's why we're so appreciative of your offer to help," she continued. "I do hope it's not too much for you."

"Why does everyone assume the job is too big for me?" Meredith asked with some annoyance. "I feel I have everything perfectly under control."

Gran looked relieved.

"Breakfast is arranged for, and the bread-baking should be no problem," Meredith stated firmly.

And in so saying, Meredith went to bed to dream of four light, fluffy, fragrant loaves of bread and a supper of chicken and dumplings, always one of her favorites.

* * *

Meredith knew she was in trouble when a smell, not a fragrance, began to seep through the kitchen and then into the rest of the house. Sniffing suspiciously, her alarm intensified sharply when Gran lifted her head from the book she was reading, and her nostrils tested the atmosphere.

About that time, Jennie flew into the front room to shrill, "Bread's burning!" Meredith hurried into the kitchen, snatched up a hot pad, and dropped the oven door. Smoke billowed out, choking her and sending Jennie racing to open the back door.

"Take it outside!" the child shrieked.

Groping blindly into the oven, Meredith managed to locate, one after the other, the four pans. With black smoke half-blinding her, she made for the rectangle of light and dumped each loaf onto the porch.

Eyes red, cheeks scarlet, hair atumble, she surveyed the ruin, speechless.

"The oven was too hot," Jennie offered wisely and was no comfort at all.

A kind hand touched her shoulder, and a kind voice said, "It's happened to all of us, my dear. It's far from easy to judge the heat of an oven simply by putting your hand inside. Now, let's start over."

So Gran led the way to the kitchen and another massive round was begun of measuring, sifting, mixing, kneading, rising, punching down, shaping, and testing the heat of the oven until it was deemed satisfactory.

From then on there was an anxious turning of dampers, adding of wood, and not a few peeks to see that all was well. When at last four loaves of sweet, light, fragrant bread were cooling on the table, Meredith felt for the first time in her life the satisfaction every cook feels in a job well done. And when Dickson Gray, with never a reference to the burned-bread smell that pervaded the house or to the four hard, lumpy brown items on the porch, asked for a second piece of bread at suppertime, Meredith's battered self-perception recovered a little.

Not feeling up to the thought of tackling a chicken,

murdering it, then eating it, Meredith contented herself with bringing up beef from the cellar and heating it for supper. Jennie agreeably helped peel potatoes, and if they were a little watery, the same restraint that kept the master of the house from complaints about the bread helped him slather the potatoes with butter and eat them with what seemed like great gusto. Besides, Meredith realized, she didn't have a recipe for dumplings. And how did one know when the stewing chicken was hot enough to add the dumpling dough?

About to dump the soapy dishwater into the slop bucket, Meredith was stopped by Jennie's squeaked interruption: "We don't put soapsuds in there, Aunt Meredith!" So "Aunt" Meredith rigidly threw the water outside, having learned that "the pigs don't like soap."

It didn't help her aggravation to find several hens pecking fruitlessly at the cannonball-like loaves of bread in the yard—or to notice the family dog with another loaf between his front paws, gnawing persistently at it as though it were a bone.

"Another thing you could do with that soapy water, Aunt Meredith," the small girl said helpfully, "is to use it to scrub the floor."

And she tramped her feet up and down, obviously fascinated by the sticky sound crackling from the linoleum's gummy spots.

16

WITH THE BREAKING OF A NEW DAY, CASSIE'S pleasure in waking was doubled by the clear summons of the meadowlark—piercing her soul with its sweetness, reminding her that not all was lost, hope endured, and happiness was still a promise.

As if roused by the bird's enticement to a new day, the babe in its "nest" fluttered and stirred. Curling herself around it for a few moments before rising, Cassie let her love reach out to her unborn child.

A double portion! she promised, almost fiercely. Enough love for Rob too!

Hungry again, and in a measure she had not known during the days on the trail, Cassie made a fire in the kitchen range, filled the teakettle, and, irresistibly drawn by the beckoning beauty of the morning, stepped outside. Here was a place of contentment, an island enclosed in an emerald sea. Man's invasion of the bush did not seem a desecration here. The snug buildings, the neat fences, the tidy layout—all spoke of peace and harmony. True, it was all rough and somewhat crude, but it seemed to fit its surroundings the better because of it. Now with a wisp of blue smoke rising from the stovepipe into the silence of the vast sky, and with the bush's arms around her, Cassie breathed the fresh morning air and felt the sun's first warmth on her cheeks to be both a caress and a blessing.

How I wish I could meet the special people who live and love here! she thought fervently.

But she could not, of course. It would take only another day or two to rest and regain both her strength and her drive and she would be on her way. Just now it was difficult to conquer the slight but consistent stirrings of uneasiness that threatened to rise from her subconscious to the light of reason: Could she find her way back to the proper trail? Did she have the physical strength for managing the oxen and the wagon again? Would Bill—Cassie struggled to recall the name of Rob's friend in Prince Albert and fought down a sense of panic when it eluded her—even be there? And how would he react to having a woman—and a pregnant one at that—thrust upon him?

If it were not for her pregnancy, Cassie realized, she might find work somewhere. But pregnant, and with some symptoms that extra care was essential to bring the child to normal term, she was sorely hampered in any effort she might make to be independent.

Pushing the anxiety down into its black and secret corner, Cassie made her way to the chicken coop. She had lured the mother hen and her chicks inside last night with a handful of grain from the sack in the granary and left the door open. If she was lucky, she reasoned, others would follow and there might be an egg or two.

The chickens were gone, lured, no doubt, into the day by the rooster's summons. Dust motes danced in the sun's rays that slanted across the straw-floored building. Reaching into the raised boxes that served as nests, Cassie was rewarded with two eggs, fresh, she knew, because they hadn't been there when she had checked the night before. No doubt there were many more secreted in the bush.

"If only I knew when you were coming back," Cassie told the unseen MacTavishes, "I could have a fresh supply for you." But the absent family had left all things well planned; their return could be delayed indefinitely without either their chickens or other animals suffering neglect in any way.

By the time Cassie had milked the cow, fed the cats, and returned to the house to strain the milk, the kettle was boiling. Pulling out a frying pan, Cassie scrambled her two eggs, warmed a biscuit from yesterday's baking, and took her breakfast into the big table in the front room.

The strong face of Andrew MacTavish looked down on her. Cassie studied it as she added marmalade to her biscuit. Older than Rob, she surmised. A man, where Rob was a boy—just a boy, and so cruelly cut down.

Cassie's upswelling of grief was stemmed when, through the open door, the meadowlark reminded her of the dream and her commitment to it.

"We'll make it, sweetheart," she whispered—a direct quote from the husband who had refused to be daunted and whose courage now lifted her head, dried her eyes, and steadied her voice.

"I hope you appreciate him," Cassie said to the smiling, sweet-faced woman in the frame on the sideboard, and then let her eyes swing again to the strong, healthy figure of Andrew MacTavish.

After Cassie had washed her dishes and put them away, she took a cup of tea, picked up Moira MacTavish's Bible, and sat down in a comfortable chair. She turned to the Book of Psalms, searching for the scrap of scripture she remembered about a "desired haven."

She didn't get past the first psalm. How apropos it was—a man blessed of God . . . "like a tree planted by the rivers of water, that bringeth forth his fruit in his season." Cassie's eyes drifted to the verdant bush; full, she knew, of life-sustaining beauty.

But "the ungodly . . . like the chaff"; and Cassie remembered the motes that drifted in the air above the straw in the chicken coop—useless, aimless, driven by any stirrings of wind or breath. Reading the passage, absorbed by the vivid comparisons, she found herself committing them to memory.

Closing the book and replacing it tenderly, Cassie realized her search for the elusive scripture would yield rich treasures. If only time allowed!

She placed her hand on her expanding middle and knew she couldn't delay her departure, in spite of the peace of her present sanctuary. And there were 150 chapters! Cassie despaired of getting through them all before common sense drove her back into the real world.

Although she had refrained from dipping into the MacTavishes' supplies (except for the eggs, and these would not keep if not used), Cassie felt a sense of obligation to them. Having checked the cellar shelves, she knew that among the jars of jam and jellies remaining after a long winter there were no strawberry preserves. She then remembered the crimson gems that flourished in the nearby meadow.

There was plenty of sugar in the cupboard, many empty jars, and good rubber rings. Taking a small pail, Cassie headed through the morning's crispness to the wild, spreading vines and there filled her rosy mouth and her pail with strawberries that she deemed were unmatched anywhere for fragrance and piquancy. Her satisfying task took up much of the remainder of the day—picking over the berries, washing, measuring, bringing in wood and keeping the fire going, boiling, stirring, filling the jars, melting wax, and sealing the fruit of her labors.

The late-afternoon sun touched the brilliant jars cooling on the kitchen table and filled Cassie's heart with satisfaction.

It will be a small thank-you and a big surprise for the MacTavishes when they come home, Cassie thought happily. She felt a pang of regret when she realized she would never know her absent benefactors.

I'll leave a note, she decided, explaining why I've been here, and thanking them.

But she felt she could never express how much it meant to find sanctuary in the little home. And how could one describe the feeling of welcome it had offered the sick and straying traveler? Perhaps she would just slip away in silence and secretiveness, as she had arrived—a closed chapter.

The following morning, which she had determined must be her last before moving on, Cassie extended her morning walk and discovered a vegetable patch. Though now overgrown with weeds, it had been well laid out and was thriving in the summer sun and rain. More and more, Cassie was of the conclusion that the MacTavish absenteeism had not been flight but was a planned and purposeful trip. The animals and fowl, the garden—all indicated the return of the couple, and perhaps soon, certainly in time to make use of the garden.

Although she hesitated over the decision to do additional canning, the abundance of green peas and their eventual loss won out. Picking slowly because of her "condition," Cassie soon had a dishpan full of peas. Finding a shady spot under a tree, she shelled for an hour, and the rest of the job was easier.

When the peas had come from the hot-water bath and she had nothing else to do except to allow them to cool and take them to the cellar to join the strawberries, Cassie turned to the Psalms again. Her heart lifted when she reached the ninth psalm and the promise "The Lord also will be a refuge for the oppressed, a refuge in times of trouble." She felt she must be coming near the haven she so much desired to read about again.

Swiftly, her eyes flew over the chapters and verses, finding that a thread of comfort and protection ran throughout: "The Lord is my rock, and my fortress. . . . he leadeth me beside the still waters. . . . in the time of trouble he shall hide me in his pavilion. . . . the angel of the Lord encampeth round about them that fear him."

Cassie put her head back and closed her eyes while the tears slid down her cheeks to drop to her bodice and onto the child—a baptism of hope and healing.

Rousing, she closed the Bible so it would not be dampened by her tears. The last thing she saw before she dropped into sleep, one slender hand on Moira MacTavish's Bible, the other on her swelling stomach, was the strong face of Andrew MacTavish, with its level gaze and open smile.

* * *

When, abruptly awakened by a sound she couldn't identify, Cassie's eyes opened, it was to look directly into that by-now-familiar face and those direct eyes.

Why, she thought irrationally, they're blue, blue as the Saskatchewan sky. Of course. And for a moment shorter than brief, she surrendered herself to the blue depths.

"Maircy! Who in heaven is it?" questioned a feminine, Scotch-burred voice.

It was then Cassie saw the woman standing just beyond the man's shoulder.

17

"GIVE OVER!" DOVIE CRIED QUERULOUSLY IN HER English parents' vernacular and snatched the milk pail out of the way just in time to avoid its being tipped into the stall. Settling herself onto the small stool again and tucking her head into the flank of the fractious cow, Dovie sighed. Things weren't proceeding satisfactorily enough to suit her where the courtship of Digby Ivey was concerned.

"You mean the courtship of Anna surely, Sister!" Dulcie had corrected when Dovie had let the unfortunate phrase slip out once before.

"Of course!" Dovie had answered crossly. It made her cross now to recall the conversation.

"Well, you can't get blood out of a turnip," Dulcie had quoted, and Dovie had frowned.

"What's that supposed to mean?"

"I mean," Dulcie said firmly, "the man isn't interested. He simply has *no* romantic feelings."

"How would you know, Dulcie?" Dovie asked. "Blood from a turnip indeed! Why, the man is a fount of feelings!"

Dovie paused to admire the assessment she had just made; Dulcie looked mutinous.

"Sister," Dulcie said boldly, "just how much do you know about men's feelings? Tell me, did Terence even so much as kiss you?"

Dovie had gasped with outrage. "Mama would have fainted to hear you talk like that!"

Dulcie persisted. "Well, did he?"

"The proprieties were observed!" Dovie said.

"Terence's bloodlessness was different from Digby Ivey's," Dulcie said thoughtfully. "I think Digby Ivey is probably a red-blooded man, all right—"

"Sister!"

"—But he hasn't been stirred into—er—remembering it. The trouble, Dovie, is with you."

"Me?" Dovie gasped.

"You! You're too—prissy. Things are done differently here on the frontier. This pussyfooting around—drinking tea—baking scones."

"So what do you suggest?" Dovie had asked her twin coldly.

"You'll have to appeal to his, er, his masculine instincts—on Anna's behalf, that is."

"Do you want to do it, Sister?" Dovie asked sweetly.

"Good heavens, no!" And Dulcie, properly set down, had hastily withdrawn her complaints and her suggestions.

The days had slipped by without any furthering of the Anna-Digby romance.

Thinking about it now, her hands methodically stripping the milk from the cow, Dovie was inclined to agree with her sister. She would have to get serious if she was to bring about the hoped-for merger.

"After all," she concluded grimly, "'faint heart ne'er won fair lady'!" Anna might not be the fairest of the fair, but she was—she was "fair to middlin'"!

As for faint heart, Digby Ivey qualified. It was a good thing that she, Dovella Snodgrass, had enough gumption for both of them!

The cow lurched again, and Dovie, always halfway prepared for this cow's problem, managed to jerk the pail out of the way with only a little milk splashed. Bossy had refused to come to the barn one bitterly cold night, or perhaps she was lost in the bush, but the thermometer had dropped so low and the wind turned so bitter that her poor tail had frozen and eventually fallen off. Now the flies tormented her cruelly.

"We all have our problems, girl," Dovie said sympathetically, but whether to herself or to the cow it wasn't clear.

While Dovie washed, Dulcie strained the milk, pouring it into flat pans to allow for easy skimming. These she covered with clean cloths and headed with them to the icehouse, a hole gouged in the earth, its pole roof mounded with dirt on which grass now flourished.

Dovie hurried to overtake her twin, preceding her down the incline to the door. Dulcie made her careful way through the gloom, settling the pans onto one of the few remaining shards of ice, blanketed in sawdust.

"Tomorrow, Sister," Dovie announced in a low voice, "I'm going to take a break from some of the outside work and make tarts."

"Mmmm—good idea."

"Not for us, Sister," Dovie said. "I'm going to take them over to Digby. Experts say the way to a man's heart is through his stomach."

"Dovie, Dovie, Dovie. You're right back to the tea-and-scones mentality! I say give up! Let's just *pay* someone to bring in the crop!"

"And how about planting next spring?" Dovie cried vigorously. "How about getting up cordwood? Cleaning the stovepipe? Banking the house for winter—have you got the strength for that? Who's going to put the wagon box on the bobsled? Can you force the side stakes into the bob-sills? Can you? And the ice—" Growing more and more heated in the cool icehouse depths, Dovie gestured toward the sinking supply. "Who's going to saw these great chunks of ice, load them, unload them, and pack them in here as though they were dominoes?"

"And for all that," Dulcie said thoughtfully, "the man is to be paid scones and tarts."

The usually placid Dovie was showing every sign of swelling like a turkey gobbler. Her rosebud mouth in her round, unlined face opened and closed, the nostrils of her small nose flared, and her breast heaved with indignation.

Before she could utter more than a squeak, a voice called down the entranceway: "I say, Miss Dovie, Miss Dulcie, Miss Anna—are you there?"

Two identical heads thrust themselves through the low, narrow door as Dulcie and Dovie peered up at the young man who looked down on them with an anxious face.

"Good gracious—it's Shaver!"

"Is something wrong, Shaver?"

"It's Pa."

After a frustrating struggle to get through the doorway, the sisters managed to exit the icehouse, pull the door shut behind them, and mount to the level of the young man. Reins in hand, he had apparently just dismounted. Or at least Dovie and Dulcie hoped so with fervency, recalling their heated conversation about his father.

Like two small, twittering sparrows the twins fluttered with concern, "What is it? Your father, you say? Has something happened to Mr. Ivey? Speak up, Shaver!"

When at last Shaver had a chance to speak up, he said, "I'm sorry to bother you, ma'ams," and then paused uncertainly in the face of what seemed unnecessary agitation on the part of his hearers and an amazing concern for a neighbor.

"Go on—don't stop, Shaver. It's no bother, I assure you. What is it, young man?"

Taking a step back from the advancing armada, Shaver Ivey continued: "Pa seems to have blood poisoning."

When the gasps had faded, Shaver added, "He's had

this sliver in his hand for a while. Well, we couldn't get it out, and now it's sort of festered, and—"

"Is there a red line running up his arm?"

"Well, yes—that's what's happening all right."

A transformation seemed to take place before the young man's bemused gaze. The sisters became all business, precision, and practicality.

"We'll come at once."

"Don't worry, Shaver."

"You go right back to your father. We'll follow immediately."

"It's a job for Anna, of course!"

"Yes, Anna. And one of us must go with her."

"You go, Sister. I'll look after things here."

"I'll go get Anna and the things we'll need. You harness the horse and get the buggy ready."

The young man, looking much relieved, stammered his thanks, mounted, and rode off.

All thought of matchmaking forgotten and with deep concern for the welfare of their neighbor, Dulcie and Dovie took the news to Anna, who rose to the occasion at once. Good, reliable, capable Anna! Dulcie and Dovie calmed themselves at the remembrance of her expertise in all crises and swiftly did her bidding as they prepared for Dovie and Anna to go and Dulcie to remain.

Flying recklessly from the yard, Epsom salts clutched in their arms along with plenty of rags and, at Anna's grim insistence, dear Papa's razor, it was a comfort to the only medical team the bush provided to hear the final words called after them by the remaining sister:

"I'll be praying!"

18

ROLLING UP HER SLEEVES WITH A PROFESSIONAL flair, Meredith felt well prepared for washday.

Sunday had been the bush homesteader's usual "day of rest." After morning chores, both inside and out, Dickson had brought the buggy to the door and helped a ravishing Meredith into it. In deference to the warm weather, she had chosen a bolero suit whose shortened jacket promised a certain relief from the day's heat while incorporating the current style. Of blue serge cheviot, trimmed all around with black mohair and silk and mixed gimp, lined with changeable silk, it still featured the newest sleeves—puff, of course; the skirt, very full, was lined with rustling taffeta and interlined with crinoline, bound with velvet.

When she was settled on the narrow buggy seat, Dickson swung himself up, only to pause: there was a scant 10 inches of space for him. Meredith gathered the spreading skirt in her hand and swept it aside while Dickson seated himself gingerly.

"Just how wide are these things?" she asked as the buggy rocked and Dickson's thigh crushed the four-yard sweep of her skirt.

"Being a Class-B buggy," Dickson replied promptly, "the seat is 27 inches wide at the bottom, flaring a little at the top, of course. You might gain a couple of inches with a Class-A."

"It's fine, I'm sure," Meredith responded faintly,

clutching her bouncing hat, "The Swell Evangeline," and its wired wings of lace and ribboned rosettes, as the rig swung from the yard.

Jennie, standing behind the seat, as seemed to be the custom with children and the only option she had aside from sitting on someone's lap, held tightly to the back of the seat and gazed with fascination at the remarkable Evangeline. Her chambray dress, giving her a deceptively demure look, billowed in the draft of their dash behind the high-spirited City Slicker.

Dickson, at Meredith's side, was certainly no country boy, she thought, noting with appreciation the fine-fitting black clay worsted Prince Albert suit, and the dashing derby worn at a jaunty angle on his black hair. Catching her critical eye, Dickson's dark face broke into a grin, and Meredith, flushing, looked quickly away.

Feeling distinctly out of place among the mostly simple gowns of the ladies of the backwoods or the much-outdated reminders of better times in earlier days, Meredith missed most of her cousin's sermon. If the women of the district studied her hat with more interest than seemed necessary, she put it down to a natural interest in fashion, never seeing the shakes of their husbands' heads or hearing the whispered "It's not the same one!"

At the close of the service Meredith found time to have a short but pertinent visit with Elva Victor, making numerous notes on a small pad of paper throughout.

Gran had painstakingly fixed the noon meal and soon retired to her room. At Dickson's invitation, Meredith joined him for a walk down the country road. Jennie had accompanied them, romping alongside, picking flowers, eating berries, and finding birds' nests.

"It's too soon to ask you how you feel about your decision," Dickson had said tentatively.

"I've had no reason to regret it," Meredith had answered quickly.

"I've wondered," Dickson continued casually, "if it might not seem a pretty big undertaking."

"Not at all. In fact," Meredith added firmly, "I quite look forward to the diversion. You know, of course, I'll be returning to the challenge of my vocation one of these days. In the meantime, a change will be—stimulating."

"Look, Daddy—gooseberries!" Jennie held out a few small, green berries for their inspection. "If we fill our pockets, we can have a gooseberry pie."

"My favorite!" her father declared and followed his daughter into the bush at the side of the road. "Perhaps Miss Meredith will make us a pie tomorrow."

"It's washday, Daddy!" the small, wise girl pronounced.

"No problem, I'm sure," Meredith called after them. "One must fix meals regardless, right?"

Now, one of Gran's aprons cinched around her waist, one of Gran's dust caps on her head, and with her sleeves rolled up in a very businesslike manner, Meredith faced washday. From a pocket she pulled a scrap of paper and the lists she had compiled with Elva's help.

"Seems straightforward enough," she thought with satisfaction. First came "Things to Assemble."

1. Wash boiler and tubs
2. Tin pail—dishpan
3. Soap
4. Washboard
5. Wringer
6. Stomper
7. Stick—broom handle
8. Bluing
9. Starch
10. Basket
11. Bench
12. Water
13. Clothes

First, she figured, the water must be brought from the well. Struggling in with the first two pails, Meredith cast a longing thought toward Emmie. Too far away to press into duty, of course, and Jennie was too small.

Setting the pails down, she found with some dismay that she should have brought the tub and boiler first. Taking a moment's breather to adjust her list and catch her breath, she was both annoyed and pleased to have Dickson come in from outside, assess the situation, and lift the galvanized tub and copper boiler from their nails on the wall, bring them in, put them onto the stove, and pour the water into them.

"Thank you," she said as sweetly as possible. "I was just about to do that."

"The reservoir is already full," was Dickson's comment. "If there's anything else—"

"No—thank you!" Meredith said quickly.

"Don't hesitate to call me if I can help."

Watching the strong back and muscular arms disappear again, Meredith quenched a dark thought concerning the bench, the wringer, and the washboard. With admirable patience, the remaining heavy pieces of equipment were located and set in place in the middle of the kitchen floor.

On a shelf in the pantry, beside the extra supplies of tooth soap, carbolic soap, Tarlo (a medicated tar soap), toilet soap, and shaving soap, Meredith found a box of "Old Glory Mottled German Laundry Soap"—"thick, fancy-shaped, hard pressed, and wrapped, made of the best material that enters into the making of strictly first-class soap," and guaranteed to give satisfaction.

"Sixty bars in a box!" Meredith barely restrained a shudder, imagining the endless washdays thus conjured up. And that would be only the beginning for anyone unfortunate enough to be dedicated to a life of housekeeping!

Lifting out a bar, Meredith devoted a good 10 minutes to its shaving. About to drop it into the washtub, she faced the empty bench and realized the tub and boiler were on the stove, *full of water.*

"No problem," she told herself, calming her irritation. Taking a pot for a dipper, she dipped water from the tub into the boiler, the reservoir, the drinking water pail, and eventually the milk pail. Even so, the remaining water in the tub on the range made it impossible for her to lift and lower it to the bench.

Just then Dickson passed through the kitchen and took in the situation at a glance—his housekeeper surrounded by pails of water, cap askew, face mutinous, and a tub half off the stove. With a ripple of supple muscles he swung the tub to the bench, bowed, and went outside, closing the door gently behind him.

Never having done so in her life, Meredith found herself quite naturally picking up the corner of Gran's apron and mopping at her face.

I believe, she said to herself, breathing deeply, I shall just have a leisurely cup of coffee while I reconnoiter.

But the teakettle was now full of cold water, and the stove top was cooling rapidly. Shifting pots around, Meredith managed to raise a lid and stuff a fresh supply of wood into the firebox. As it began to take hold and flare, she went back to her list: "Keep fire going!" she added, underlining the instruction with a wicked slash of the pencil.

Still hopeful of completing the task with finesse, she turned to the heap of soiled clothes. She gingerly picked up a cumbersome pair of greasy overalls and started a pile of "dark clothes—very soiled." This was followed by "dark clothes—slightly soiled" (a small batch indeed, so she compromised and added towels to this lot). "White clothes" she divided by soiled, slightly soiled, dainty, and rags. "Colored clothes"—

The silent form of little Jennie filled the doorway, hair half combed, shoes unbuttoned, an obviously old and faded dress buttoned crookedly, her nightdress in her hand.

"Over here," Meredith said, pointing to the slightly soiled white batch. With a pitying look, the child looked the piles over and dropped the gown (which Meredith could now see actually had small flowers on it) into the "colored clothes—slightly soiled" pile.

Jennie looked hopefully toward the washday clutter on the table. Breakfast! Of course the child would be hungry; Meredith had completely forgotten the sleeping Jennie.

Sweeping aside the bluing bottle and the package of starch and the soap shavings, Meredith invited the little girl to sit down.

"What would you like for breakfast?" she asked, regretting it as soon as it was uttered.

"Pancakes, please," Jennie said promptly.

Pancakes. Meredith had forgotten to ask Elva for a recipe for pancakes.

"How about a nice egg?" she offered brightly.

Jennie studied Meredith thoughtfully. "I s'pose that will be all right," she said finally. "Poached, please."

Simple enough, Meredith thought with relief. Filling a frying pan with water, she set it over the hottest lid, got an egg from the pantry, and as soon as the water was boiling briskly, cracked the egg and dropped it in. To her dismay, the egg white scattered amid the seething liquid, floating off in all directions.

Staring at it dumbly, she looked down to see the small face of Jennie beside her, studying the situation gravely.

"The water must not be boiling when you put the egg in, else the white breaks up. But that's all right, Auntie Meredith," the little girl said kindly. "I'll eat it anyway."

Somehow Meredith tipped the water out into the slop pail without losing the egg. Managing to work a cake turner under it without breaking it, she lifted the egg toward the plate Jennie had set in front of herself. There was no toast.

The big eyes of the little girl looked up at her. Carefully Meredith returned the egg to the pan, placed the wire toaster over the stove lid, cut a slice of bread, and watched tensely as it toasted. Then, placing it on the plate, she brought the egg, the yolk now firm and half cold, and placed it before the child.

Jennie studied it for a long time. Then, "Thank you," she said doubtfully and picked up her fork.

Meredith, jaw clenched, returned to her washday list: "Fix breakfast for latecomers."

Now it was back to dipping water, this time into the tub on the bench. Next she added the soap shavings, then the first batch of clothes—white, slightly soiled, of course. And she felt good about her decision.

Slightly soiled or not, the stomper required using, and before she was through with the first batch, Meredith's back ached and her arms were weary. With the aid of the old broom handle, she lifted each piece from the water and somehow thrust them into the wringer, which Jennie obligingly turned after warning, "Auntie Meredith, a basket! They're dropping on the floor!"

With the "white clothes—very soiled" came the increased effort with the washboard. Even so, when they were lifted out to the wringer, they appeared dingy even to Meredith's unpracticed eye.

"These are s'posed to be boiled," Jennie offered and pointed to the boiler of water on the stove. "And I think something goes in there to make them white, like sal soda or vinegar or ammonia or something."

"I'm sure boiling will do very well today," Meredith decided in a choked voice and proceeded to carry the wet towels and dish towels and sheets across the linoleum to the waiting boiler, drop them in, stoke the fire again, and let them boil. Her hair drooped, her shoulders ached, her face flushed, and her temper shortened.

By the time Meredith reached the "dark clothes—

slightly soiled," the floor was awash, her apron soaked, her sleeves wet, her nose shiny, her eyes glazed.

Looking at the scummy rinse water and listening to a helpful Jennie saying, "Vinegar added to the rinse water will cut the scum," her nerves weren't calmed with the appearance of Dickson. It was dinnertime.

With a swift look around, Dickson cleared his throat and said, "I think I'll just make myself a sandwich. I often do that on washdays."

Jennie's scandalized eyes opened wide, and her hand flew to her mouth. "Daddy! You told a lie!"

Dickson had the grace to look uncomfortable as he made his way past his daughter into the pantry. There he slapped some bread and meat together and escaped, stopping only long enough to check the coffeepot. Finding it empty, he took a drink of cold water from the dipper.

Numbly, Meredith finished the "colored clothes—very soiled," finding the heavy coveralls too heavy to go through the wringer. With Jennie holding one end and Meredith the other, they twisted the bulky garments until they were ready to be taken out and hung on the line along with those that had preceded them.

Finally, about to empty the water and clean up, Meredith caught Jennie's eyes on her once again.

"Well," she said, "what is it?"

"Leave one pail for mopping the floor," the child said humbly. "The soapy water—use it to scrub the porch with the broom. And—"

"Yes, go on."

"With the old broom, swish out the toilet."

19

"MAIRCY ON US!" THE STARTLED VOICE EXCLAIMED, jolting Cassie from what she felt must be another of her dreams.

But the voice was real enough, coming from over the shoulder of the man bending over her. The blue eyes in which she had lost herself momentarily were very real too, and now they were filled with concern.

"Come, lassie," the man said reassuringly, "there's no need for alar-r-rm." In him too the Scotch burr was evident, though not to the degree it was in the woman.

Pressing back into a corner of the chair, Cassie stared at the couple, rational thought having forsaken her. How could she explain her invasion of their private domain—being perfectly at home in their home?

If she had known it, her instinctive reaction, wrapping her two hands in a protective gesture over her unborn child, spoke directly to the hearts of the hearers. The man's blue gaze, a patch of Saskatchewan sky, dropped to Cassie's bulging abdomen.

"Tell me your name, lassie. Mrs.—"

"Quinn," Cassie managed. "Cassandra Quinn."

"And I'm Andrew MacTavish."

Of course you are, Cassie thought. It was the one thing she was certain of in this startling moment. Andrew Mac-Tavish, in person, was the sturdy, healthy, vigorous man he appeared to be in the pictures. Just now his hair, sandier than she had imagined, fell across his broad forehead from under the edge of a cap that had crushed and fitted itself to his head and had been pushed to the back at a casual angle.

But the woman, surely she was not the Moira Mac-Tavish Cassie had almost come to believe she knew. Almost as tall as the man and almost as sturdy, and with the same sandy hair, lightened with gray, her face was broad and kind—and definitely old.

Noting Cassie's appraisal of the older woman, Andrew MacTavish said, "This is my aunt, Allis MacTavish."

"Moira," Cassie began. "That is, Mrs. MacTavish—" And perhaps her disappointment showed in her voice.

"Far away, with loved ones in Ontario," the man said, his voice echoing her disappointment.

Cassie made as if to rise, and the man, touching her shoulder lightly, encouraged her to remain seated.

"Sit still, Mrs. Quinn," he said, "while we get ourselves settled here a little. After all," and his strong white teeth gleamed briefly through a smile, "you weren't goin' anywhere, it seems."

Cassie fell back, making a small attempt to salvage some dignity for herself. "Well, yes, I was—in the morning—"

"You can tell us all aboot it soon enough. Now, Aunt, just carry your bag in here. I'll carry in all the rest and put them away."

Cassie, head back, eyes closed, heart hammering, listened to the homey sounds of the snug cabin's inhabitants and envied them.

And tomorrow, she thought despairingly, I'll go and never feel these arms around me again. Surely she meant the warmth and protectiveness of the home itself, never having felt a flesh-and-blood embrace since Rob's death.

Booted feet tramped back and forth, doors opened and closed. Someone lifted the lid on the kitchen range and chunked in the firewood she had chopped and carried in, filling the woodbox, intending to leave it full—another puzzle for the homecomers.

"The kettle's hot, Aunt," the man's voice said. "Why don't you make tea? When it's ready we'll all sit down and find oot what the problem is with the wee lassie."

"Look, Andrew," the Scotch-touched voice burred softly, "there's fresh bread and new butter."

Cassie had started the bread early in the day, thinking ahead to her departure and the need to carry supplies with her. Covered and cooling, it sat beside the butter Cassie had churned from the cream she had skimmed from the milkings of the past few days.

"What a fine welcome!" the man said appreciatively. "Saves a lot of work this first night back, eh, Auntie?"

"It would have been bannock, laddie."

"Next time," the nephew said, and Cassie could hear the smile in his tone.

While the tea steeped, Andrew MacTavish seemed to be showing his aunt where things were kept; to Cassie it seemed the Scottish woman had never been in the house before.

"Everything is in its usual place and as tidy as we left it." The man's voice indicated his surprise. "Perhaps she's not been here long. Although the bread and the butter and the wood—"

"It's all as neat as a pin. I think Moira would have approved of this young lass's car-r-re of her-r-r things."

"Bring the tea, Aunt, and I'll bring the food."

Miss MacTavish came bearing the familiar brown pot and three cups, all old friends to Cassie. Andrew carried a tray containing the rough old breadboard with a loaf on it half cut in lavish slices, the mounded butter in the treasured butter dish and a freshly opened jar of Cassie's strawberry jam.

Setting the tray down, the man looked at Cassie speculatively. "Seems, lass, you've been busy," he said. He indicated not only the bread and butter but also the jam glowing ruby red in a shaft of the late afternoon's sun.

"A little thank-you," Cassie said humbly. "There were so many berries—the meadow smelled sweet with their crushing after the animals walked over them."

Andrew MacTavish's gaze seemed to watch every nuance of expression on Cassie's face as she talked, and she found herself blushing. What would he think of her?—so bold, sitting in apparent content in Moira's chair, as if it were her own, and clutching Moira's Bible.

Her eyes fell to the worn black book, and Andrew MacTavish's eyes followed hers. Lifting it gently, he placed it back into its position on the small table in front of the window, with Moira's picture stationed beside it.

"And have you needed its comfort, lass?" he asked gently.

"More than I can say," Cassie responded in a small voice, "though I'd like to try to express it."

"And you shall, ver-r-y soon."

Allis MacTavish poured the tea, and Andrew manfully slathered butter and jam on the great slices of bread, set them on plates, and handed them around. Dainty linen serviettes were plucked from a buffet drawer; serviettes Cassie had no more than touched lovingly with her fingertip.

"It seems, Mrs. Quinn, as though you've lived in our wee hoosie for a while—"

Cassie dropped her head.

"—and have left hardly a ripple to reveal you were here." His burr, Cassie noted, came and went; she had an idea he was a second-generation Canadian and had never personally seen the braes and lochs of the old country.

"And you were plannin' to be gone tomorrow, slippin' away like a shadow?"

"It was time," Cassie answered simply. "My oxen—they're in the pasture—brought me here. I'll never completely understand why—"

Her voice grew thoughtful. "I've wondered if it was—fate."

"Fate?" Andrew MacTavish glanced at the Bible. "Had you been prayin' aboot it, perhaps?"

"Oh, yes, I certainly had," Cassie said with surprise. "You see," she continued slowly, "I was on a search—in a way."

"A search?"

"For—for the place Rob, my husband, and I had in mind all the way here." Cassie could not bring herself to mention the "desired haven" of her heart's hunger, a haven, she thought with a catch of her breath, she had begun to believe she had found—only to learn it belonged to Moira MacTavish.

"And Rob?" the man asked in the gentle way he had, while his aunt replenished the teacups.

"Rob?" Cassie could not know her expressive little face went as still and lifeless as a winter landscape. "I left my Rob on the prairie."

Allis MacTavish bent her kind face over the back of the chair and laid her weathered cheek on Cassie's head.

"Ach, my wee one," she murmured, "donna fret yoursel'. All's well—you'll yet see it's so."

Taking a deep breath, Cassie told in simple words the story of the dream of a homestead in the West, of the long trek, Rob's illness and death, her dogged persistence in continuing.

"It's not that I'm brave or anything like that," she said in a burst of self-revelation, and never knowing how gallant she appeared. "I just didn't have any other choice but to hitch up and head out." Cassie revealed the hopelessness of her situation and the courage that had been like a thumb in her back against terrible odds.

"You see," she finished as if it explained it all—and it probably did—"there was Robin to consider."

Again her hand, childlike in its shape and strength,

spread in a maternal gesture as old as time itself over the babe in her body.

"Do you mean," Allis MacTavish asked, "there's no one waitin' for you—lookin' for you, in Pr-r-rince Alber-r-rt?"

"Not really. Rob thought a friend of his might be there."

Over Cassie's head the young man and his aunt exchanged looks of unbelief.

"Wheesht!" the woman whispered, and the man's craggy Scotch face looked grim.

"And now, if you don't mind—," Cassie said with dignity, struggling to her feet in anything but a dignified manner and bringing a quirked smile to the face of the watching man, "I'll just go outside and—check on the kittens. I know you have many things to say to each other."

She made her way across the room, through the attached kitchen, and out into the evening's long-fading light. With the kittens tumbling about her feet, Cassie went to the fence, leaned her arms on the top rail and her chin on her arms, and looked at the meadow spread out before her. She knew its fragrance, its berries and grasses and flowers, its birds and some of its insects. She knew its rippled pond, its nests and ducks. She knew its dew by early-morning light and its afternoon warmth on her bare feet. She knew its meadowlarks.

The evening's first star shone no brighter than the tears that shimmered in Cassie's eyes.

"Tomorrow," she told the distant Bib and Tucker. "Tomorrow we'll say good-bye."

20

WITH CLODS OF EARTH FLYING FROM UNDER THE horse's hooves (hooves on which each shoe fit tightly and snugly), Dovie was stricken by a feeling of reproach for her plot to entice a good and innocent man into undertaking a task that was so contrived. Now it seemed the height of frivolousness.

She clasped the Epsom salts a little tighter and offered thoughtfully, "Sister, life is so much more than meat and drink, don't you think?"

Anna turned from giving her attention to the reins, to consider this astonishing bit of philosophy from her ordinarily featherbrained sister. Catching Anna's speculative glance, Dovie enlarged on her thought.

"The vicar's sermon [the Snodgrass family persisted in using the English title for their pastor] reminded us that life is so much more than food or raiment. And yet we spend most of our time worrying about them."

"Bush people know the bitterness of having too little of each. One can't blame them for being desperately anxious, even desperate, at times. Not everyone has been here as long as we have, or is as well settled."

"And still people keep flooding in—as if this were the Garden of Eden!"

Anna nodded. "For some it is. They've left persecution and poverty behind, and if they can hold on, they'll have the new beginning they dream of."

"It's that holding on—some folk are getting off the train where there's no depot, maybe a boxcar for a station, no station agent, no one to tell them where to go or what to do."

"And probably not speaking the Queen's English!"

"No food supplies—mail uncertain. Ending up on land with not enough cleared space to put a tent, most like. Cooking over a campfire until they can get a shack up—subsisting on bannock and stew that is mostly potatoes and rabbit—"

"Even gopher!"

"And no doctor, Anna! No wonder you're as busy as you are. You've sewed up ax gashes, chopped-off fingers, and goring by bulls. You've lanced more boils and mustard-plastered more chests than I can shake a stick at!"

"And now here's our neighbor, in serious trouble."

"Because of a sliver! You know, Anna," Dovie said thoughtfully, "such trouble makes us think of things in a different light. As for me, I'll never look at a loose horseshoe in quite the same way ever again."

"Loose horseshoe? You've lost me this time, Sister," Anna responded, looking confused. "Loose horseshoes are not to be sneezed at, I can assure you."

Dovie abandoned the subject, resigned to the fact that she couldn't express what she meant without giving herself away. But one thing she knew: Digby Ivey needed them as much as they needed him.

What a salve that realization was to a conscience threatened with self-reproach! And what fuel it added to the fire of her zeal! Anna would be so right for Digby!

Dovie clutched their bag of the catalog's numerous remedies and pleaded silently, "Hold on, Digby! We're coming with hope and health and happiness!"

* * *

The lamp in the middle of the dining room table touched the graying head and earnest features of the minister with a gentle blessing. Glancing up from the books spread before him, Gerald Victor rubbed his hand over his eyes and said, "Have you enough light there, my love?"

Elva lifted her head and smiled at her husband. "I've been wondering when you'd come back to the land of the living. I've got enough light for this rough darning, thank you. Would you like a cup of tea before we go to bed?"

"I think I would," Gerald said, stretching. "I'll just gather my books and papers and clear up here."

When they were both comfortably seated, nibbling a ginger snap and sipping tea, Gerald asked, "What did Meredith have on her mind? Seems a long walk in the middle of the week for a social call. Is she getting along all right?"

"I think it was a good thing you had to make that call on old Sister Dunphy," Elva said. "She came on purpose to talk about household matters, obviously needing some help."

"No! Not that I'm surprised that she needs help, but that she'd ask for it."

"She didn't admit to having any trouble, Gerald."

"She wouldn't. I remember her as being a very independent child. Of course, she was raised with every convenience—even had a nanny of sorts before her parents died. Then her uncle and aunt continued the coddling."

"At least she had enough gumption to get out and try to do something with her life."

"Oh, she has gumption, all right. And grit—I have to give her that. But is it enough for the bush?"

"Well, we'll see, won't we? I notice she's still wearing that locket with that man's picture."

"The one busybody Emmie asked to see? And then asked all sorts of questions about?"

"The boss's son. Something went wrong in that relationship, Gerry. And Meredith seems to be trying to prove something, maybe to herself, perhaps to him, by her insistence that she can do the work at the Grays'.

"Did she come to complain or to plead for help of some kind?"

"Just to ask questions—and to make lists. That girl lives by her lists! The trouble is, Gerry, I can't describe all the details that crop up to make a simple list a farce.

"It's cleaning day that has her worried. But even with her lists of 'things to assemble' and 'things to be done,' she hasn't included things like keeping the fire going constantly, being sure there's plenty of water in the pail and the reservoir, keeping the teakettle and the woodbox filled, having dinner cooking while you're working and having supper in mind. She'll have to stop occasionally and tend to Gran's needs, and little Jennie needs supervising. All these things and more will upset her routine. She can't begin to foresee every emergency."

Gerald just shook his head.

Elva sipped her tea and thought about Meredith's list of "things to assemble":

1. Cleaning cloths
2. Ammonia
3. Furniture cream (And if they don't have it, Elva thought, she doesn't have the recipe for it.)
4. Feather duster
5. Rug beater
6. Broom
7. Kerosene (And when I told her about picking bedbugs off the mattress creases and dropping them into a can of it, the poor dear actually seemed to blanch, Elva thought.)
8. Soap and water
9. Basin and pail
10. Mop
11. Apron and dust cap

"I shudder to think what sort of list she'll make when I tell her how to get a chicken from the pen to the pot," the preacher's wife said reflectively.

21

C LEANING DAY!" JENNIE SAID BRIGHTLY, LOOKING
expectantly around the faces at the breakfast table.

Gran's face looked troubled. Dickson's expression was guarded.

Meredith's lips tightened in spite of her effort to keep her face impassive. That child! she thought with some annoyance. It's almost as if she taunts me with it.

But Jennie's next remark put that suspicion to rest. "I'll help, Auntie Meredith. I'm awf'ly good at beating rugs. I can do them as soon as I gather the eggs and feed the chickens."

"And I'm sure I can take care of washing up the breakfast things," Gran offered. "The hot water will do my hands good."

Dickson cleared his throat and toyed with his eggcup. "Please," he said cautiously, "don't feel you have to—ah—overextend yourself with cleaning house. We've muddled along for quite a while, and we'll be content with things as they are, if need be, until Miss Janoski can get here and dig into the heavy jobs that have been neglected. Gran just wasn't up to spring cleaning this year."

"I trust we shall not be greatly hampered by the absence of the estimable Miss Janoski," Meredith said crisply. "It's true, no doubt, that the woman has devoted her life to home matters while I have sought a higher goal, that of serving my generation through affairs that affect many lives. While I cannot say that I come to this task with the same noble purposes and, yes, passion, that I invested in the world of business, still, the same mental capacity is available and shall, I am confident, be sufficient."

Jennie stared, hypnotized, at the all-but-impassioned face of the speaker. Gran's mouth fell slightly open. Dickson, unfortunately, took that moment to experience a fit of coughing. His dark-complexioned face, or what could be seen of it above his serviette, flushed darker still as he struggled to get his breath.

Rising quickly, Meredith stepped around the table and, with a small but capable fist, pounded the unfortunate man soundly between the shoulder blades.

"Now," she said brightly when Dickson emerged, watery-eyed and breathing deeply, "Miss Janoski couldn't have handled that little emergency any better, wouldn't you agree?" And her fascinated audience could only nod speechlessly.

Rising with some haste from the table, Jennie carried the remnants of underdone toast to the kitchen; Gran emptied far more coffee grounds into the slops than were necessary. Dickson, bringing in pails of water that he wouldn't have ordinarily, looked around helplessly and, with a quirked grin at his grandmother (who put her finger to her lips and shook her head), turned and went out to his day's work. But not before he had noticed, with mixed feelings, the determined face of his "housekeeper" under Gran's dust cap, her long-lashed gray eyes unflinching between escaping wisps of auburn curls. Her mouth, so made for smiles and laughter, he thought, was set in a firm line as she studied her list and began to assemble her cleaning needs.

Turning back before he stepped over the sill, Dickson said, "Remember: if I can—"

"Help," Meredith supplied for him and waved him on. "What other women have done I can do." (And do better, her tone implied.)

"Unbelievable," he muttered and was startled when Jennie, lugging a pail of eggs, asked, "What's unbelievable, Daddy?"

"This day, for one thing," Dickson responded immediately. He put his hand on his daughter's shoulder, and they stood on the porch, surveying the beginning of a bushland country day. Birds lent flashes of brilliance from every tree, their songs giving cheer to all who had an ear to listen. The more distant sound of chickens and turkeys and a few ducks and geese added a not-unpleasing counterpoint to the morning madrigal. In the distant field new calves romped on awkward legs. Overall, the great Saskatchewan sky stretched its blessing.

Looking up, Jennie caught a look of perfect contentment in her father's face. Young as she was, she understood it.

"It's beautiful, isn't it, Daddy?" she asked, needing to share his moment.

"Yes, love, it is. And I'm so glad we're here."

Breathing, feeling, absorbing together, the minutes passed. Then, "Better get on with our day," the man said as he bent to hug the slender little body so dear to him. He tipped his hat to her gravely and strode toward the barn.

Watching the little intimate scene through the screen door, Meredith felt a mist of tears in her eyes, and when the little girl set her pail on the porch and came into the kitchen, Meredith greeted her with a gentle "Do you want to go play, Jennie? You may if you wish. I'll manage—somehow—without you."

"First things first, Gran always says," Jennie said wisely. "Besides, Auntie Meredith, you might need me."

Moved by an impulse she had never known before, Meredith gave the child a hug. "You're right, honey," she said, "I just might. Now where do we start?"

"We could do cobwebs," Jennie suggested hopefully.

Although "air bedding" was first on Meredith's list,

she agreed to the cobweb procedure. While she was hesitating, Jennie fetched a worn, clean pillowcase and inserted the broom into it.

"What a clever girl!" Meredith complimented. "I'll get a piece of string to tie it to the handle."

"You don't tie it, Auntie Meredith," Jennie said patiently. "Else you couldn't pull it up and down and back and forth to find a clean place for rubbing the walls."

And indeed the makeshift duster soiled quickly. With no spring cleaning after a winter's smoke and grime, not only were cobwebs beyond the reaching of Gran's stiffened shoulders, but ceilings and walls were sooted and yielded a patina that quickly smirched the cloth. Jennie eventually turned the pillowcase inside out, Meredith taking a turn when the small arms tired.

"I love doing the cobwebs," Jennie declared.

Loved doing the cobwebs! Loved housework of any kind! The very idea was startling.

"There!" Jennie finished the task with satisfaction. "Now we'll put the pillowcase in the laundry . . ." And her voice trailed off at the stricken look on her "aunt's" face. Could one ever love doing the laundry? Meredith thought not.

While Jennie gathered the small braided rugs from around the house, took them outside, and beat them—another task she apparently "loved"—Meredith moved into the front room. Here a Brussels carpet, somewhat worn, decidedly needed a cleaning. Gran graciously left the area for the outdoors.

With effort, Meredith moved aside the furniture, only to realize she could never carry the rug—probably six by eight feet—outside to the line. Sweeping was the only procedure. Hips swaying in rhythm with the vigorous sweeps of her arms, Meredith wielded the broom robustly, surprised to find herself humming under her breath and almost—almost enjoying herself.

A shadow across the floor caught her attention. Pausing in her energetic attack on the rug, she looked toward the doorway through a cloud of dust. Dust danced in the sun's shafts of light; dust rose in clouds around the room; dust settled in drifts onto the furniture. Dust drove the startled face of Dickson Gray back a hasty step.

Regaining his composure in a masterful manner, Dickson hastily explained, "Came in for—er—something to eat."

Dinnertime! And he had kindly refrained from taunting her with the truth. Perhaps it was dust, but Meredith felt quick tears sting her eyes. It *is* dust! she determined instantly. Dust or humiliation!

"I'll just fix myself a sandwich," Dickson said kindly.

"You will not!" Meredith said fiercely, remembering that he had done the same on washday. "Give me a few minutes."

Beating the dust from her clothes (unfortunately forgetting the smudges on her nose), Meredith hastened to the kitchen to find the fire low. Fighting down a mounting hysteria—half laughter, half sob—she built up the fire and, while the stovetop heated up, mixed a batch of pancakes, cracked eggs, and sliced bacon. Then, juggling three pans on the wide stovetop, she flipped pancakes and fried bacon and eggs. The pancakes were tough, the bacon frizzled away to a curly knot, and the eggs, which had started out to be over-easy, broke in the turning and ended up scrambled.

Of course there was no coffee when at last the miserable meal was on the table and Gran and Jennie called to eat.

"It's a meal for milk!" Dickson declared on the spot. And again Meredith felt threatened by a bewildering rush of tears.

When the meal was over and Jennie was doing the dishes, Meredith crept into the front room to survey the damage, to find Gran dusting off her rocking chair and seating herself calmly.

"I know," Meredith said despairingly. "I forgot the dust covers."

Gran raised faded eyes to the dejected face and reached a gnarled hand toward Meredith. With a smothered sob, Meredith flung herself down at the calico-covered knee and buried her dusty face in Gran's lap.

"You can't be expected to know everything it took me a lifetime to learn," Gran said gently as she stroked the vibrant auburn hair now released from the confining cap and cascading from its loosened pins.

"You mean you made a mess of things too?"

"I remember burning holes in most of my Dick's white clothes, trying to bleach them with lye—a mistake we could hardly afford in those days. I remember blackening the whole house with smoke when I forgot to open the damper. I remember serving my family saskatoon pie that tasted more like buckshot than anything else. I remember—"

"Enough!" Meredith said with a shaky laugh, raising her face, streaked with tears. "Then what, Gran, should I have done about the rug?" she asked.

"Tea leaves sprinkled all over it—used, damp tea leaves—keep the dust down," Gran said, again gently.

"And I've been throwing ours in the slops!"

"I know." There was a hint of laughter in the old lady's voice, and again Meredith felt the betraying prick of tears behind her eyelids.

"You can substitute torn-up, shredded newspaper," Gran suggested, "and with a good dusting everything will be as right as rain again."

Sitting up, Meredith pulled a crumpled "list" from her apron pocket. "Look at this," she said and presented the paper for Gran's scrutiny.

In silence Gran read:

1. Polish furniture
2. Clean piano keys
3. Wash windows
4. Mop kitchen floor
5. Wash bric-a-brac
6. Scrape grate
7. Blacken range
8. Fill lamps
9. Clean lamp chimneys
10. Organize kitchen shelves

At this point Gran folded the paper. "My dear," she said compassionately, "clean up this front room, dust the rest of the house, do the kitchen floor, and call it a day."

"But—"

"But nothing. Dickson shall fill the lamps, Jennie shall clean the chimneys. The bric-a-brac and piano keys and windows can wait."

When the prescribed tasks were done, a simple supper of macaroni and tomatoes, new peas, and a fresh-from-the-garden lettuce salad was topped off with a fruit dish of strawberries with thick cream. Dickson settled back contentedly with a cup of coffee. When Gran smiled at her with an air of victory, Meredith felt a sense of accomplishment to compare with nothing she had experienced previously. That evening she wrote:

Dear Aunt and Uncle,

You'll never imagine the day I've had. Cleaning day on the frontier is an experience! But I plowed through and came to the end of the day feeling pretty good about it all. That is, until I was emptying the scrub water and Jennie advised me to use it to scrub the outhouse. I had begun to feel things had gone swimmingly when Gran went to bed and reported I had forgotten to bring the bedding in from the line . . .

Leaning away from the table and the letter, Meredith

stretched her back and arms and felt again the mix of despair and satisfaction that had marked her day, and she wondered at it.

"Have a cup of tea to finish off the day," a masculine voice said and set a cup before her.

Meredith looked up into the fine, dark-visaged face bent above her and was struck by the sympathetic look in the black eyes. Uncalled for, a vision of another face—superior in its expression, adamant in its denunciation of her skills—flashed before her, the first time she had thought of Emerson Brandt all day.

Thoughtfully, Meredith took the proffered cup.

"I believe," she decided silently, boldly, "I shall murder a chicken one day soon and serve it with dumplings."

22

A S EARLY AS CASSIE WAS UP, ALLIS MACTAVISH had preceded her to the kitchen. A breakfast of porridge was waiting when Cassie made her appearance. Bowls of it appeared on the table as soon as Andrew stepped into the kitchen to set down the morning's milk and wash his hands.

From the high warming oven Miss MacTavish lifted a plate of crisp toast made from Cassie's bread, picked up the coffeepot in her other capable fist, and beckoned toward the table in the "room." Humbly, Cassie took a place indicated, realizing she was, after all, only a guest. Looking around at the objects grown dear to her, it was hard to force them into a casual place in her heart. In spite of herself, a sob shook her small frame; with an effort she caught and silenced it in her throat before it could burst forth and betray her.

"Everything looks pairfect," Andrew MacTavish was saying, unfolding his serviette and placing it over his lap. "The creatures in the pasture ha' done well, just as I supposed they would, and I got back before Daisy had her calf. Your oxen," he said, turning to Cassie with a smile, "are makin' themselves r-r-right at home." And his Scottish burr rolled charmingly.

Just like me, Cassie thought, seeing ever more clearly her presumption in availing herself of the MacTavish homestead's bounty and beauty. At the time of her arrival—heartsick and wracked with bodily pain—it had seemed a God-given gift, satisfying her heart's need and healing her body's pain.

Unfolding her own serviette and placing it over her knees, Cassie noted wryly that her lap had all but disappeared. Robin, too, had thrived.

When she raised her eyes, Andrew had opened a book —the Bible, she saw with surprise—and was riffling the pages.

"We'll start Paul's letter to the Philippians," he explained and began reading.

"Grace be unto you, and peace, from God our Father, and from the Lord Jesus Christ . . . making request with joy." Certain phrases sang in Cassie's ears and lingered.

"Confident of this . . . that he which hath begun a good work in you will perform it until the day of Jesus Christ."

The deep voice read on a few more verses, but Cassie was caught and gripped by a startling thought: Had He begun a good work in her—and was He, even now, performing it? The possibility was awesome in its scope, startling in the horizons it opened.

Her wanderings—had they not been aimless? Was there, after all, a Master hand that guided storm-tossed souls to blessed havens? And if so, would that "good work" continue?

Cassie recalled her bitter night of weeping in her lonely wagon bed and the first tendril of hope that had lifted from the ashes of her dreams toward the sun—the Son! Lost in wonder, she suddenly realized that Andrew MacTavish, sandy thatch of hair bowed and eyes closed, was praying.

"Our Father, we thank Thee for bringing us safely home again and for Your care of all things while we were away. Bless, we pray, our absent loved one, and bring her back to us again ver-r-y soon. Thank You for Aunt Allis and her goodness in comin' to help me in the meantime.

"And Father, bless this wee stray that Thou hast

brought our way. And may we minister to her as Thou would have us to do.

"And now, Father, we thank Thee for Thy provision and the bush's bounty. Bless this food to our day's strength, and may we honor Thee in all we do. In Jesus' name we pray."

And Andrew helped himself generously to the rich, thick cream from his own cow and lathered the butter of his own farm's making onto his toast, covering it with jam made from berries that ran riot in his own meadow.

The talk was general until Allis said, "How often do you go to the post office, Andrew? I'll be worrit until we get wur-r-d of Moira, whether there's been any improvement since we left."

"I don't go often, Aunt, but others do, and they drop off mail all the way home. As soon as Wildrose knows I'm back, this will resume, I'm sur-r-re."

"Wildrose—," Cassie said, "—is that where I am?"

"You mean, lass, you haven't even known where you were?"

"As I said—I was so sick and half in and half out of my senses, I didn't even know when the yoke of oxen left the proper road. Wildrose . . . ," she finished dreamily.

Cassie's eyes lifted to the window and the glorious morning breaking over the land. Fragrant with odors she couldn't identify—and probably never would after she moved on, she thought fleetingly—it was pure enticement. That it bore the dainty fragrance of the wild rose, she suddenly felt achingly sure.

"Moira—Mrs. MacTavish," she said, turning back into the conversation, "I gather she is—ill?"

"Not really ill, lassie. Just verra delicate. But she has the heart of a lion," Andrew explained. "When she knew my heart was set on homesteadin', she pluckily gave me her full support. I couldna ha' made it withoot her. But, in the process, she just aboot wor-r-re hersel' oot."

"You must miss her terribly."

"I do, lass—I do. We're verra close." Andrew's eyes seemed to look far beyond the small room, to someplace where it was fixed in fond love on the distant absent one.

"I'm her-r-re temporarily, lass," Allis MacTavish explained. "I canna stay all winter. It's hoped that in two months or so, darlin' Moira will be strong enough to come home. 'Til then I'll bide wi' my laddie." And the aunt gave the "laddie" an affectionate look.

"It's verra hard for a man to make it alone, lassie," Andrew said. "There are those who do, but often they quit, or get oot. Hopefully they can find some lassie who'll ha' them. For a *woman* to make it alone—" Andrew's tone turned grim.

"I know," Cassie said quietly. "But I have no choice, you see. It's Robin and me—against the world. And we'll make it! Having come this far—we'll make it!"

"Your dream of a homestead—," Andrew pursued. "Wives of pioneers are equal partners with their husbands, no doobt aboot that! But, lassie, they don't ha' equal rights on the homestead, sad to say. A single woman, lass, canna obtain a fr-r-ree homestead."

Cassie heard him in stunned silence.

"That will change someday—it has to," Andrew assured. "Women, workin' side by side with their husbands, are demandin' equal treatment. And their husbands, for the most part, back them; I cairtenly do. We must gr-r-rant our women the vote! But for now—," Andrew shook his head, "—a single woman must purchase her land."

Tears of disappointment, dismay, and fear for the future threatened as Cassie heard the death knell of her dreams. "Excuse me, please," she whispered and made her escape.

Stumbling toward the pasture fence, Cassie leaned her arms onto the top rail and gazed blindly into the beauty spread before her. Some dim and distant perception felt the warmth of the morning sun on her head and arms, breathed in the rare mingling of grass, flowers, strawberries, and bush. She heard the homey sounds of a calf's bawl, rustling leaves, and bird song mingling with the ruder sounds of a hen celebrating its achievement.

To have come so far, only to have her hopes and dreams dashed so cruelly and so finally!

The burden of the past weeks overcame even Cassie's intrepid spirit. Dropping her head onto her arms, she let the tears flow freely. "Oh, Robin, Robin—what shall we do?"

Strong arms slipped around her sob-wracked body. Cassie turned, like a bird to its sanctuary, to the strength and comfort of the generously offered shoulder, and she wept on it.

"There, there, lass," Andrew comforted, rocking her as a mother would a babe. "There's no need to cry in this way."

"My dreams—my plans—my future—," Cassie cried wildly.

"Dinna weep more . . . ," Andrew crooned over and over, until finally Cassie quieted.

Turning from the haven of his arms, Cassie choked out a broken, "I'm sorry—," and exchanged the warm arms for the support of the cold fence rail.

"I've been enough of a burden already," she managed. "Please don't pay attention to my weakness of the moment. I'll be fine, I'm sure, and on my way soon—"

"Na, na, lass! That's what I came oot here to talk to you aboot! Aunt Allis and I have been talkin' things over, and we'd like it if you'd just stop her-r-re with us—at least until after the birth of the bairn."

Cassie lifted startled eyes to the concerned face, so masculine in structure, so honest and honorable in expression, guileless and open, and found herself thinking, What a good man he is! Perhaps—can it be—it's the Jesus in him? For of one thing Cassie was sure: Andrew MacTavish knew well the Lord to whom he prayed.

The sun, climbing high in the sky, seemed to touch the young face lifted to it with a certain tenderness. That it also mercilessly revealed the dark shadows under the tear-misted eyes and turned to gold a smatter of freckles on the straight little nose, Cassie could not know. But she saw the play of expressions across the man's face as he looked down on her silently for a few moments, and she wondered.

"You don't have to make up your mind today, Cassie," Andrew said quietly. And he turned her toward the house.

To stay in Wildrose! The very possibility of it set Cassie's thoughts awhirl. But—could she accept the generosity of these people without contributing? Her funds were limited—barely enough, she figured, to get her to Prince Albert and keep her through the birth and until she could decide her future.

Even this, it seemed, the Scotch pair had considered.

"You see, lass," Andrew was saying, matching his steps to hers, "the busy time is here—weedin' the garden, puttin' away the vegetables, pickin' berries, cannin', washin' all the winter beddin'—and on and on. And then there's the daily workload of meals and the care of the animals and fowl and such. It's just too much for an auld lady like Auntie. She'd be much relieved to have you stay and help."

Cassie noticed his lapse from his slow rolling burr, a sign of his earnestness, and appreciated him for it.

Aunt Allis pulled them into the house. "Well, lassie, what aboot it? Will ye stay and give an auld lady some help?"

Too overcome for words, Cassie's face apparently spoke for her, and Aunt Allis wrapped the smaller figure in a massive embrace.

"And we'll seal the bargain wi' a cup o' tea!"

And once again they all sat around the table, emptying the teapot and making plans for the day and the coming weeks. Almost immediately Aunt Allis invited Cassie to call her "Aunt," and they all agreed to a first-name basis.

Andrew unloaded Cassie's wagon, storing her treasures and household goods in a shed and bringing her personal things into the house. The wagon was put under a shed roof, and she could almost feel its sigh of relief to have its torturous journey ended.

"But just temporarily," Cassie told it silently, watching with a curious pang as Andrew greased it well in anticipation of a day when it would once again creak its uncertain way northward.

"The fairst thing to do," Aunt Allis announced with great good cheer, "is to wash our dairty clothes!" And with one will the two women began the necessary sorting, while Andrew filled the tubs and the boiler before leaving—obviously with a glad heart—for his farm duties.

"We'll do some special, extra task each day," Aunt Allis planned, talking as she worked. "One day we'll put up carrots, another day we'll go berry pickin' and make jelly, or, mairciful heavens!—wash the quilts. That, along with regular-r-r jobs, like ironin', cleanin', churnin', bakin', cookin', should keep us oot of mischief!"

Aunt Allis didn't seem to expect an answer, so Cassie made none, reveling rather in the routine—the normalcy— the very "hominess" of their task. It seemed like a dream! —but, Cassie acknowledged realistically, a dream from which she would awaken shortly.

"I thought," Aunt Allis was saying, "we'd get Andrew to buy some flannel and bits o' ribbon the next time he goes to town. We'll wor-r-k in the evenin's on things for the wee bairn."

Cassie nodded happy agreement.

"Moira's sewin' machine will be put to good use. Andrew insisted on gettin' it for her-r-r. I declare—that lad canna deny her anything. He's that fond o' her-r-r! He does his ver-r-y best to make her life aisy."

And after that spate of tongue-rolling gymnastics, to which Cassie listened, fascinated, Aunt Allis subsided.

"How do you think she'll feel about me being here, Aunt Allis—someone using her sewing machine and all?"

"You'd have to know our Moira, lassie. If there ever was a saint on airth, it would be her-r-r. Andrew adores her-r-r, and so does everyone who knows her-r-r. You'd love her-r-r, lass. Never worrit—she'll be happy to have you here. Hoots! Somewhere along the way fooks began callin' her-r-r Lady Moira!" Aunt Allis' voice softened. "And silly as that may seem, lass, it's a title that fits. There isn't a more gentle craiture in the wor-r-rld than our Lady Moira!'

Later, passing through the "room" to the bedrooms with an armful of sun-sweet clothes, Cassie stopped to study again the sweet, mysterious face of the absent Moira.

"Lady Moira—," she breathed and felt humbled in the face of such an honor.

But, Cassie thought doubtfully and blushed to consider it, how would any woman feel to have another woman, especially a young one, in close quarters with her husband? The pictured, gentle gaze followed an uneasy Cassie across the room as she stored away the clean linens and wondered if, in deciding to stay in Wildrose, she had made a decision of the head or the heart.

23

WHEN ANNA AND DOVIE PULLED INTO THE IVEY yard, Shaver was awaiting them. With a bound of youthful energy, he was out the door to take the horse away to the barn and unhitch her.

"I'm sure glad to see you!" he said, almost exploding, as if pent-up emotions had finally found an outlet. His boyish face began to relax from the strain that had twisted it.

"Everything will be fine," Dovie said soothingly with an assurance she couldn't feel. If the poison had gotten into the bloodstream . . . "Don't worry, Shaver. With Anna here—"

"Stop clucking around, Sister," Anna said matter-of-factly, turning to the house with her curatives. Dovie followed with the food they had wisely thought to bring along. No telling what kind of cupboard two bachelors maintained!

Digby Ivey sat in the kitchen with his injured arm before him on a simple kitchen table. But the table was scrubbed until the boards gleamed white. Breakfast dishes had been cleared away and washed and were draining in a dishpan. The room was cheery and bright with crisply clean curtains, a shining floor, and a spotless range.

Dovie had her first doubt concerning any desperation driving Digby Ivey into the arms of a woman, even one so capable as Anna. On the other hand, what a pair they would make!

But Digby needed help, and laying all plotting aside, Dovie joined Anna at the side of the afflicted man.

"Excuse me for not rising, ladies," Digby said with a small attempt to make light of the problem. "But one doesn't rise to one's—angels of mercy." His eyes were very bright, and his cheeks flushed more than the wind-and-weather patina he usually wore.

Anna clapped a hand to the man's broad forehead and removed it with an expressionless face. "Hot water, Dovie," she said calmly.

"It's hot," Digby said, to no one's surprise, certainly not Dovie's.

"Of course it is!" she muttered, and noted with a sigh the neat stack of snowy towels set out and awaiting whatever treatment Anna prescribed.

Anna's neat dark head was bent over the swollen hand; the fatty area at the base of the thumb was turgid and ugly.

"Where did you pick up the splinter?" Anna asked sharply. "The barn area?"

"The woodpile," Digby answered. "It should have been no problem—but I shoved my hand pretty forcefully under an armload I had just split and rammed a piece in pretty far. Didn't go in at a slant, unfortunately; it seemed to go straight in. I dug around at the tip that showed, but it broke off and, dig as I would, I couldn't get hold of it. It's in the right hand, you see, and my left hand is too awkward to do much. As for Shaver," Digby explained, "his prodding around in there did more harm than good, I think, though he did his best."

Carefully Anna unpacked Papa's razor, the best money could buy, its hollow ground fine steel winking wickedly as Anna opened it from its fancy celluloid handle.

"Lay the blade in the water, Sister," she instructed, "and try and keep the handle out; I don't know how much heat that celluloid will take without melting."

Anna placed a towel on the table and laid Digby's

arm, palm up, on it. Methodically, she organized the materials she would need, most of the abundant supply ordered through the catalog.

Anna's bag was stocked with worm pills, sarsaparilla ("undoubtedly the best blood purifier in the market . . . try a bottle when you feel out of sorts"), female pills ("a combination of pennyroyal, tansy, cottonroot bark in concentrated form . . . very powerful and required to be used cautiously"), carbo wafers ("a true specific for sour stomach, heartburn, and distress after eating"), headache cure ("one or two doses will relieve the most obstinate case of nervous headache in 10 minutes"). There were little liver pills ("for anyone inclined to biliousness"), pink pills for pale people ("for all diseases arising from mental worry, overwork, early decay, etc."), and microbe killer ("if taken once or twice a day, will prevent la grippe, catarrh, consumption, malaria, blood poison, and all disorders of the blood . . . this preparation will eradicate any form of disease and purify the whole system").

"Ahhh," Anna breathed and lifted this last bottle from among its neighbors.

A little more sorting among toothache wax, nerve and brain pills, herb tea, camphorated oil, and guaranteed cures for dropsy, epilepsy, general debility, brain fag, summer colds, croup, and scrofula, and Anna, with some relief, located a bottle of laudanum, identified as "tincture of opium." One more foray into the bulging bag, and Anna located the package of Epsom salts.

Shaver had come in and stood, mouth agape, at the array of lotions, potions, pills, and draughts that were available nowadays for most any ailment. But his sense of relief obviously faded when Anna brought the razor blade from the pan and gripped it with mastery.

"Here, Shaver," Anna said, indicating his presence was needed. "You can help support your father. Dovie, take his other side. Now hold tight."

Shaver's young, open countenance paled, but he stepped forward gamely enough, stationed himself at his father's right side, and gripped the arm. Dovie, feeling helpless, took Digby's scrupulously clean but calloused left hand in hers—just why, she didn't know; if Digby were to give a massive start in reaction to the pain Anna was about to inflict, Dovie knew her meager hold would be sluffed off as quickly as a fly from the back of a horse.

Taking a stand across the table, Anna gripped the swollen hand with her left hand and with her right hand held the razor poised for the slash that would open the distended pad for the prodding that must be done. Digby Ivey closed his eyes; the jaw line tightened under the blue-black whiskers.

"Dear Digby," Dovie managed to say urgently before the blade descended, "trust yourself to Anna!"

At what cost the patient remained rigid against the slicing and the probing that followed could only be imagined; Digby's face, building to dark red, paled to gray, while drops of perspiration formed and ran. But no sound escaped the tight lips, and no muscle jerked in the taut body, even though the exploring and excising continued until, at last, Anna was satisfied she had removed every bit of foreign matter.

Even then the pain continued. Anna squeezed the gaping wound gently but firmly, until the discharge ran red with all pus swabbed away. Dovie loosened her trembling hold, reached for a towel, and mopped Digby's brow, his cheeks, his throat. "There, there," she found herself crooning. "It'll be all better now, dear, dear Digby."

With a great breath, Digby let his muscles relax and his head fall back; Dovie was there to cradle it with her comforting embrace while Anna cleaned the wound and placed a pad over it.

"Now," Anna said, "we must get that poison dissipated quickly." She proceeded to fill a basin with warm water and dispense a goodly amount of Epsom salts into it.

"Shaver, you and Dovie get your father over into that comfortable rocker," Anna instructed, "where he can lean back a bit while he soaks his hand."

Shaver moved a small table up beside the patient, Anna set the basin on it, and she soon had Digby's hand to soak. While Dovie brought a quilt from a nearby bedroom and wrapped it tenderly around the big body, now shaken at times with an occasional tremor of reaction, Anna cleared away the signs of the surgery from the kitchen table and put the bloodstained towels to soak.

At dinnertime Anna heated the pea soup they had brought with them, sliced bread of Digby's baking, and applied butter of Digby's churning. She brought it to her neighbor, and Dovie spooned it into his mouth, tenderly wiping away spills and proffering bite-size portions of bread from time to time.

The sisters' ministrations continued all afternoon. As chore time approached, Anna made preparations to go home.

"You'll need to stay on, Dovie," she said. "Alternate the soaking in water with warm compresses. Before I leave, Shaver can get his father into bed."

When this was done and Digby showed signs of drifting off into fitful sleep, Anna touched a hand to his forehead again, shook her head, and departed, leaving explicit instructions with Dovie concerning careful dosages of laudanum, to be given only in modest doses for pain and to ensure rest.

Shaver took care of the chores, stepping into his father's room from time to time to turn anxious eyes on the flushed face, ask if there was anything he could do, and leave, to bumble about the kitchen eventually, stirring himself up some supper and offering some to Dovie.

Digby seemed disinclined to eat but sipped thankfully of the liquids—tea and water—that Dovie faithfully dispensed, slipping an arm under the graying head and raising it to her shoulder while she held the cup to his lips.

"Is Anna gone?" Digby asked, rousing himself. "I didn't get a chance to say thanks—"

"Anna understands, dear Digby—Anna understands," Dovie soothed. "She'll look after you. Never worry. Anna is on the job! Dear, good Anna." And Digby, apparently reassured, drifted off again into a laudanum-induced ease.

Shaver could not be persuaded to go to bed. Leaning back in the rocking chair, he dozed uneasily, rousing himself to keep the fire going and the water hot. Dovie—seated at Digby's bedside, changing the hot compresses, offering sips of water, and bathing the damp forehead—watched and waited.

Holding the good hand in a comforting grip and watching the face with its lines of suffering, Dovie made a shocking discovery: England and Terence Amberly seemed a million miles away and a thousand lifetimes ago. Unwrapping the compress, Dovie leaned over the arm, the light from the bedside lamp picking out the worrisome red line.

With a sob, Dovie slipped to her knees, laying her gray-touched fair head on the lump that was Digby Ivey, and wondered what she would do, what Anna would do, if their efforts were to be of no avail. The farm and its needs faded into unimportance beside the worth of the man.

"O Lord," Dovie prayed, earnestly and most fervently, "don't let this good man die. Let him finish out his life and know the happiness and fulfillment that are still available to him."

Her tears made a damp spot on the coverlet. Placing her head on her arms, Dovie drifted into an exhausted sleep.

Just when Digby Ivey's big hand was placed tenderly on her bowed head, she never knew.

24

DEAR UNCLE HOMER AND AUNT MARIE:

They say confession is good for the soul. And my soul needs help in the worst way tonight. You are too far away for me to see your smiles at my expense or to hear your gasps of dismay, so I will make my confession before I go to sleep. That is, if sleep will come; my mind is awhirl with the day's activities.

First off, I got ahead of little Jennie's usual announcement concerning what workday it was by saying, "I think we need a hodgepodge day—a day to catch up on all the odds and ends of things we've overlooked." Jennie looked doubtful, but game.

After we washed the windows inside and out (by the way, Aunt, did you know a solution of one quart of water and three-fourths cup of ammonia makes windows shine?), I determined to make tapioca pudding. The trouble was, I didn't know the tapioca needed to soak in water for 24 hours. Consequently mine turned out to be the first pudding in the history of the West to be *chewed*. (By the way, Aunt, did you know a goose egg-sized hunk of lard equals three-fourths of a cup? Not that I put lard in the tapioca pudding, mind you. No, it went into the dried apple pie. Aunt, here's a good rule of thumb for pie crust: half as much lard as flour; half as much water as lard. These dimensions, aside from "getting the feel of it," are all a person needs to make pastry. Just how long it takes to get the feel of it, I can't say. But the apples were tasty.)

When Mr. Gray took off for a trip to Meridian and Jennie went with him, I became very daring. This is a good time, I thought, to have a chicken dinner, and to fix it without little Miss Know-It-All breathing down my neck.

I looked in on Gran, and she was dozing; it seemed like the kind hand of fate. At least at the moment.

I tell you, Uncle and Aunt, one's mind goes into a tailspin when one is in a chicken coop surrounded by dozens of chickens with beady eyes and bobbing necks. But because of the press it wasn't hard to grasp one, which I did by plunging my hand amongst them and grabbing the first leg I felt. The creature came upside down with a great fuss, beating its wings wildly and causing a hubbub in the barnyard.

It absolutely refused to keep its head on the chopping block! I ended up giving a great hack every time its neck came near the block, but it *would* keep on twisting and squirming and squawking, until—more by good luck than good timing—hatchet and neck met. Met and parted!

I dropped the poor, battered bird into the sawdust. To my horror it still didn't give up! With a great flopping and jerking it resisted still, even going so far as to spurt blood in a wide arc over the woodpile and me.

When I had finished throwing up, I collected the hen and took it to the porch. After a great deal of yanking and hauling, I got the feathers mostly off (if you wish to do this, Aunt, I suggest you dip the hen in scalding water; that way you can do what is called "plucking" without tearing the skin off. Skin is essential if one is to hold one's chicken together in one piece for baking). I also understand that the small, downy feathers ought to be saved for making bed pillows, etc. And never, I repeat, *never* throw feathers into the stove.

The blaze this made would have been great for singeing off the tiny pinfeathers that defy plucking. But, of course, all this was forgotten when Gran made her startled appearance in the doorway, holding her nose in her poor gnarled fingers. (When cooking onions, Uncle and Aunt, set a tin cup of vinegar on the stove and let it boil; this doesn't guarantee, however, that a *burnt-feather smell* will dissipate.)

When I could get back into the kitchen, I faced the most challenging part of the job: disemboweling the carcass.

I knew there were things in there that needed to come out—"innards," they're called. Obviously, they weren't going to come out through the neck opening. So I made an incision in the nether region, closed my eyes, inserted my hand, and pulled. (Until now I hadn't paid much attention to the gender of my bird. One should either butcher scrawny old hens or fowl of the male variety.) The first thing I pulled out was a full-sized egg, very soft-shelled, but ready to be someone's breakfast very soon. This was followed by decreasingly smaller eggs—tomorrow's and tomorrow's and tomorrow's. 'The pigs will enjoy these,' I consoled myself as I discarded them into the slop pail.

There are unspeakable things inside a chicken. I understand now it is a good idea to wash in there with water to which a small handful of soda has been added. Oh, well—I'm sure cooking destroys everything inedible. And I will say I cooked my chicken thoroughly. So thoroughly, in fact, that it fell from the bones (as I said, it needed skin to hold it together).

When, at the supper table, I put a tureen of it in

the middle of the table, Mr. Gray said, with great good cheer, "Ah—chicken soup! Nothing like it!" I gave him, I suppose, a withering glance, for he subsided, adding weakly, "Or whatever you call it."

"What *do* you call it, Aunt Meredith?" Jennie asked.

In a flash of pure inspiration, I said, *"Chicken Emerson."* It needed only a little salt (and some thyme and possibly some onions and carrots and potatoes) to make it quite a remarkable dish. Certainly nothing Emerson Brandt need be ashamed of!

That, followed by our apples (scraped out of the crust, they were quite delicious), finished our meal. Mr. Gray, declaring that the fine meal called for celebrating, finished off with a can of apricots purchased that afternoon at the Meridian store (12 cents a can or $1.25 a dozen—an extravagance, with green gage plums at 9 cents).

I do trust my dreams are not filled with visions of flopping, headless chickens. By dawn's early light (and crowing time), I'm sure I shall wonder why I hadn't made it a rooster . . .

At that very moment one of the chickens fortunate to have escaped the day's hatchet set up a turmoil in the chicken yard. Laying aside her pen, Meredith pulled back the curtain and peered out her bedroom window toward the source of the furor. Something, it was clear, was causing a disturbance—perhaps a skunk. To her surprise, Meredith found herself filled with indignation: how dare such a creature invade the peace and tranquillity of her hen house!

Hastily snatching a wrapper from a hook, she pulled the bunglesome affair over her nightgown, aggravated by the yards and yards of "latest-style foulard percale," with puff sleeves, of course, that now seemed outrageously monstrous, "neat turned-down collar, three rows of fancy serpentine braid across bust and back, forming yoke; back with plaited effect from yoke to waist; girdle belt, collar, sleeves, and belt trimmed with serpentine braid." To add to the bulk of its "lined-to-waist full skirt and wide hem," it featured the popular "full Watteau back."

Now struggling with the long piece of material that hung down her back, train-like, from neck to floor, Meredith wondered just who in the world this "Watteau" person was and what gave him the right to inflict this silly style on women! With his insignia flying behind her, Meredith sailed down the narrow stairs, across the house, through the kitchen, across the porch and the yard to the hen house. Somewhere along the way she was joined by the family dog, and together they swept into the churning melee to catch sight of the striped back of the interloper as he slipped under the far side of the pen and made his escape into the night—but not without leaving his calling card.

Reeling, breathless, choking, Meredith tottered from the chicken yard, eyes stinging, nostrils burning, throat gagging. Before the amazed eyes of Dickson, Gran, and Jennie, Meredith made straight for the horse trough and tumbled herself—Watteau train and all—into the water.

Numerous scrubbings and rinsings later and with stacks of wet towels piling heavenward in the moonlight, Meredith, wrapped in the sensible folds of Grandpa Gray's hastily located teaseldown cloth nightshirt, made her way back upstairs to the privacy of her room, wondering if the smell of mothballs wasn't as bad, after all, as that of the skunk.

Just before her door closed, she heard Jennie, on her way back to bed, say cheerily to her father, "Well, we can't smell the burned chicken feathers anymore."

25

THE SUN-FILLED, RAIN-BLESSED, PEACE-TOUCHED days slipped away as summer spilled her bounty lavishly abroad from field and meadow, garden and bush. Never had Cassie been busier; never had she worked harder. Never had she been more contented.

And lived out before her daily was the grace demonstrated in the life of the man Andrew MacTavish. Gentle he was, but wholly masculine; kind, but not condescending; patient, but filled with humor. He was undoubtedly a serious Scotsman, but never a dour one.

And when, at their morning devotion time, he read the phrase, "The life which I now live in the flesh I live by the faith of the Son of God, who loved me, and gave himself for me," Cassie felt she caught a glimpse of the Source of that life. Surely Andrew MacTavish dwelt in the "desired haven," both physically and spiritually.

Cassie watched as he paced the boundaries of his physical haven and saw his satisfaction and contentment. And, watching, she felt like an interloper—a bystander warming her hands at another's campfire, her heart at another's dream.

The tender ties of the MacTavish dream enfolded her in a grip that threatened to become unbreakable. Here was peace, here was security, here was love. Cassie absorbed it without meaning to, reveled in it like a thirsty person relishes a sip of pure water—and, finally, fought against it.

Finding herself dusting the tall banquet lamp that graced the center of the table and tracing its embossed moss roses and leaves lovingly, she put it from her firmly, reminding herself it was not hers, but the absent Moira's. She polished the fragile spoons with their gracefully engraved initial "M" and laid them back in their plush-lined case as if they burnt her fingers. The dainty lace edgings on serviettes and pillowcases were constant reminders of the loving hands that had crocheted them.

Cassie's own loving stitches went into a layette for Robin. True to her word, Aunt Allis instructed Andrew concerning what sort of material to purchase and how much, and in the long summer evenings the two women cut and sewed, talked, and, in Cassie's case, dreamed.

But the dream insisted on taking the shape and form of the MacTavish homestead. Desperately, Cassie conjured up a place of her own, hers and Robin's. But the dream's outline was vague, its dimensions unreal; its fulfillment escaped her for the present reality, a reality that did not want to let her go to insubstantial dreams.

The desired haven for Cassie assumed the proportions of the snug log house in the district of Wildrose in Saskatchewan's bush. It was as simple—and as complex—as that.

And though Andrew and Allis talked as if Cassie and Robin were permanent members of the family and seemed to take it for granted that Cassie would stay on even after the birth, Cassie knew, and knew with a desperate urgency, that she must leave—and must leave as soon as possible. Robin would be born in a few weeks, before winter came and the roads were impassable, and Cassie would leave immediately. She would—under no conditions, she maintained almost passionately to herself—be here when "Lady Moira" came home to pick up the threads of her life, a life Cassie found herself envying against her will.

But a letter from Ma Bates was chilling. Cassie had

written to Ma to give the sad news of Rob's death and to inquire into the whereabouts of Rob's friend, Mike Barber.

"Cassie girl," Ma Bates had written laboriously, "I'm sorry to tell you that your grandma has passed on. She didn't live long after you left, poor soul—may she rest in peace. And Mike Barber, last time he wrote, told me he was leaving Prince Albert to go to the Peace River country . . ."

Cassie had folded the letter and put it away under the uneasy gaze of Andrew and Aunt Allis. They should not know, she determined fiercely, that her outlook was so bleak.

"I'll need to be on my way," she said briefly, "as soon as Robin is born." And in spite of their protests, she left it at that and made plans to drive on as soon as she was able to travel again.

It became more important than ever to hold onto the dream of reaching her "desired haven." Consequently, she viewed the visit from the district's minister as a God-sent opportunity finally to locate and perhaps understand the scripture she clung to so stubbornly.

Andrew was away when "Brother" Victor arrived. He was met at the door by Aunt Allis, who invited him in after he had introduced himself.

He inquired about Lady Moira's health, and his praise of the absent Mrs. MacTavish was warm and sincere. "We've all missed her," he assured Cassie and Allis. "She teaches a Bible class for our ladies when she's here, and we've found no one to replace her. Fine people, the Mac-Tavishes."

Allis MacTavish excused herself, hastening to the kitchen to make tea for the visiting pastor. Taking a deep breath, Cassie looked into the man's kind, intelligent face, and asked quickly, "I wonder if you'd be so kind as to help me—"

"Anything—you've just to ask," the man said warmly.

"There's a bit of scripture—that is, I know some of it, but I can't find it in the Bible. It's where God is promising a haven—I don't remember much more than that."

"There are very few scriptures using the word 'haven.'" the minister said thoughtfully. "Tell me—was it from the Book of Psalms?"

"Yes, it was! And I've been looking for it—"

Picking up Moira MacTavish's Bible, the minister thumbed quickly, saying, "Then I know exactly where it is. In fact, it's one of my favorites. Ah, here it is—Psalm 107—" And he read the familiar words.

"But you need to read verses 23 to 30 to get the picture," he explained. "This describes souls that are melting because of trouble—reeling, staggering—"

"That's the one!" Cassie breathed.

"Like a ship in a great storm at sea, at wit's end about what to do or where to go."

"Yes—yes—"

"Then they cry to God and He brings them out of their distress; He makes the storm a calm and brings them into their 'desired haven.' The Bible tells the reaction: 'Then are they glad because they be quiet.'"

Cassie herself was quiet, absorbing the beautiful promise.

"The 'desired haven,'" the pastor continued, "may mean different things to each of us. But it surely means peace and quiet where there has been turmoil and distress."

Aunt Allis came in with the tea tray and though Pastor Victor asked Cassie if there was anything further she wanted to talk about, she assured him there was not and turned to the tea and tarts with a full heart.

"And how long do you think you'll be with us, Miss MacTavish?" the pastor asked.

Cassie heard Aunt Allis's response with a sinking heart.

Aunt Allis hesitated. "I haven't had a chance to talk to Cassie aboot this," she said, "but per-r-r-haps this is a guid time. You see, I've had wur-r-d that my auld mother-r-r is not doin' sae good and needs me. It looks like I may be havin' to leave ver-r-y soon."

The pastor expressed his regret, offered a brief prayer, and took his departure. But not before Aunt Allis loaded him up with fresh cream and butter and a jar of Cassie's strawberry jam.

Silently, Cassie helped clear up the tea things, while Aunt Allis enlarged on her mother's age and infirmity and her dependence on her daughter's care.

"I had hoped to get through the winter-r-r," the Scotswoman said with a sigh, "but I'll have to go as soon as arrangements can be made."

And I'll have to go before then, was Cassie's chilling decision. There's no way I can be here with Andrew alone.

But Andrew, when he came in and learned that Aunt Allis had broken her news, completed the picture.

"Auntie," he said, looking into Cassie's still face, "surely you told her—"

"Och, laddie—I forgot! You see, lass, Moira's comin' back!"

It was not good news to Cassie. She couldn't understand the despair that welled up, nor the tears that threatened. The thought of watching the happy reunion, of being an uninvited observer and reluctant participant in the couple's pleasure in each other's presence, was not to be borne.

Perhaps seeing something of this in Cassie's eyes, Andrew took her two hands in his and held them surely against his chest, looking down in Cassie's upturned face with compassionate eyes.

"Lass, dinna think o' leavin' us," he said swiftly. "You'll surely bide wi' us through the winter."

Cassie made an attempt to pull her hands away, unable to bear the gaze that seemed to look into her very heart. "I cannot stay!" she cried silently. "I cannot stay and —God help me—I cannot bear to go!"

Andrew seemed to read the inevitable in Cassie's face. With a sigh he loosed her hands and, as she turned away, said strongly, "Well then—y' must stay through the birth o' the bairn."

When Cassie said nothing—*could* say nothing, Andrew continued, "I'll not let you go before then, lassie. T'would not be the thing to do, at all. I'll ha' to refuse to let you yoke up the oxen," and though his voice had a smile in it, his eyes were serious. "Please," he continued gently, "put up wi' us, for Robin's sake."

"Oh, Andrew, it isn't that!" Cassie cried, turning to him earnestly. "It isn't putting up with you! Never that!" But how to express the pain that impelled her to leave, or the sense of necessity that drove her to make the decision. To remain—with Andrew MacTavish and his lady? Impossible.

But she knew the wisdom of Andrew's decision; it would be foolishness to think of trying to make Prince Albert and its uncertain future until after the child was born. How much longer? Two—three weeks. Oh, hurry, Robin! Hurry! Two weeks till birthing, two weeks till traveling is feasible. A month—please, God—one month—

But Allis was cutting her hopes to tatters: "Moira is on her way, lass. She'll be here next week, and I'll be leavin' for Ontar-r-rio."

26

IN DOVIE'S DREAM SHE WAS BACK IN ENGLAND. Amid much cheering and confusion, she was kneeling to be crowned queen. The weight of the great crown was pressed down onto her head, and while Big Ben bonged unendingly and the massive crown bent her painfully earthward, Terence Amberly besought her to remember him and to make him king.

Coming awake with a start, Dovie was to hear the old mantel clock striking five, its *choing, choing,* competing with the equally unmusical sound of two or three roosters calling up the dawn. Raising her hand to her groggy head, Dovie encountered the warm flesh of Digby Ivey's hand laid in a sort of benediction on her tousled hair. For a moment, before moving, Dovie felt like a queen indeed, royally crowned.

Fully awake at last, she gently lifted the inert hand, laid it on the bedspread, raised herself from an awkward crouching position to her knees, and cautiously looked toward the still-sleeping figure of Digby Ivey.

With a joyous heart she recognized Digby's usual high color, but free of the flushed tinge that had been so obvious the night before. His chest rose and fell slowly, and his breathing was even and light.

Whispering a prayer of thanks, Dovie remained in her cramped position, wondering at herself and her huddled oblivion at the side of her patient. Then remembering, she put one hand to her head, and her eyes sought those of the immobile man. Those eyes were open and fixed intently on her face.

Still on her knees, "It's me—Dovie," she said quickly. "Anna's gone—but she'll be back."

"I know Anna's gone," the man said.

"You thought I was Anna—and you're grateful to Anna—"

"I am grateful," Digby said, and his hand, so near hers on the bed, covered her own. Warm, pulsing with life, the hand enveloped Dovie's completely. The rooster crowed, the mantel clock ticked on in a distant part of the house, and time stood still.

When it seemed that life would go on—though whether the same ever again Dovie could only wonder—she took her free hand and sought the pulse in his wrist.

"Normal—it's—it's normal," she managed, under the intent look that never wavered from her face.

"I wouldn't have thought it was," Digby said. And indeed, its usual steady, rhythmic beat was not behaving normally. There was an irregularity to it that strangely matched her own, for Dovie could feel her heart moving in an unusual pattern in her breast.

"Digby," she said urgently, anxiously, "it's Dovie! Are you truly awake? Do you think you're in some—some kind of fever?"

"Perfectly normal, just like you said," Digby assured her.

Getting hastily to her feet, Dovie placed a hand on Digby's brow; it was cool and—praise the Lord—normal indeed. But his pulse, under her hand, was definitely erratic.

"I think," she said cautiously, "you may be having some sort of reaction to the tincture of opium—although it's very mild and perfectly harmless when dispensed according to directions. Are you quite sure you feel all right?"

"Never better," Digby said. "In fact, I haven't felt so good in a long, long time." His hand tightened.

With considerable alarm, Dovie managed to free her hand and wondered why it tingled so. Asleep, no doubt, from its awkward position . . .

"Now you just keep calm," she murmured placatingly, "while I go and get some coffee started."

Dovie escaped, closing the bedroom door behind her and leaning her trembling form against it. Regaining some of her composure, she crossed the room to shake Shaver awake and made her way to the kitchen—and normalcy.

When Shaver had clattered his way outside with the milk pails, when the kindling had caught and the fire was crackling in the range, when the coffee had been measured and put to boil, when her hair had been straightened before the small kitchen mirror and her rumpled apron exchanged for a fresh one, Dovie turned toward the bedroom to find Digby standing in the doorway, dressed and vigorous, watching her.

"Digby! You mustn't—"

"Of course I must. I'm fine. The red line is gone—" And Digby held out the arm, his sleeve rolled up for Dovie's inspection. "Of course the hand is sore and I'll have to get Shaver to help me with certain buttons and perhaps with my shaving," he ran his good hand over his dark beard, "but I'm on the mend, thanks to—"

"Anna! All thanks to Anna!"

"I was going to say 'God.' I heard your prayer last night, Dovie. And, of course, thanks to Anna. And to you."

Again that curiously intent look that put Dovie's knees into a most unaccustomed tremble. The man was undoubtedly affected by the experience he had been through. And oh, it was too bad to have to insist on rational thought when the irrational was so—so appealing!

"Come, Digby," Dovie managed, pulling out a chair at the side of the table. "You need sustenance. Your natural resources are out of order."

Digby gave a great laugh. "Dovie, Dovie! You are just too precious for words! It's all part of your charm."

But Dovie was weeping.

With perfectly healthy legs, Digby strode across the small kitchen and with very normal masculine arms wrapped the small disconsolate figure against himself.

"Why—now—what's this?"

"Oh, Digby! You're so obviously out of your head! And I just can't bear it! It's so—so cruel—to hear these things and know you don't know what you're saying— what you're doing! I'm trying to understand."

"Come, love—," Digby began, and Dovie wept anew. To slip inadvertently from "Dovie" to "love" was so painful—and so natural. How could he make such a slip?

But Digby was seating himself and pulling the forlorn bundle onto his lap, where it cradled in what seemed to be utmost despair.

"Anna—," she began one more time, on a hiccup.

"What about Anna?"

"Anna—Anna—Digby. Have you thought about Anna for—a wife?"

"Dovie, love—" (It sounded so perfectly ridiculous— and so perfect!) "I don't need a housekeeper—or a nurse. Let your heart rule here, Dovie, not your head."

Digby Ivey's face filled with tenderness. Then, slowly, sweetly, and very deliberately, he bent his head, set his firm lips onto hers, and thoroughly kissed her—thoroughly kissed the lips that in almost 40 long, empty years had never been kissed before, lips that knew instinctively how to respond, so that when Digby lifted his head and pressed her wet cheek to his chest, a light glowed in his eyes and a prayer of thanksgiving welled in his heart.

* * *

"You see, Sister," Dovie said wonderingly to Dulcie in the privacy of their bedroom, "he never did consider marrying Anna, in spite of all we did."

"*You* did, Sister."

"Well, yes," Dovie admitted. "Not that Anna appreciated it!"

"In fact, she was quite *irate* when she found out."

"For shame, Sister!" had been what Anna had said. "How could you?"

But Dovie, in light of how things turned out, didn't regret the misdirected wooing.

"I never would have had the gumption to do it for *myself*," she admitted to Dulcie, "but for Anna I was quite bold."

But even to her twin, Dovie couldn't share the intimate things Digby had said: "Anna's a dear, and I love her—as a sister-in-law. But you, my love [and how Dovie's barren heart had blossomed at the word!], fill my need for sweetness and gaiety and laughter. I have everything else a man could need, except loving companionship, and this you bring me in full measure.

"And as for the farm—" Digby's eyes twinkled and Dovie had the grace to blush, "we'll work something out where the work is concerned."

"You see, Sister," Dulcie said severely, "it doesn't pay to be scheming and underhanded!"

But Dovie wasn't so sure. Having had such phenomenal success the first time, she was inspired to suggest, "There's still Morton Dunn, Sister! If you're interested, I could—"

"Stop it, Dovie!" and Dulcie put her hands over her ears and blushed fiery red. "I'm perfectly happy just the way I am! And if I should ever change my mind, I'll do my own husband hunting!"

"But, Sister, I can hardly *bear* to think of going off and leaving you—after all these years together!"

"Nonsense!" Dulcie said firmly. "You'll be just a few miles away. I'll have two homes now! And anyway, at long last I'll have a bedroom all to myself."

The sisters hugged and cried, but they were happy tears.

"What about Terence Amberly, Sister?" Dulcie asked eventually.

"Terence who?" Dovie responded smartly, and they fell into each other's arms again, with gales of laughter.

"I've been fooling myself for years," Dovie said honestly. "Perhaps it's been a sign, Sister, of the need I have to love someone and to be loved—in that way."

"Married—right after harvest!" Dulcie marveled and opened up a whole new line of conversation.

* * *

Shaver welcomed having a mother. Barely recalling his own mother, who had died when he was very small, he entered into the excitement of the occasion by proposing numerous titles for the new one, "Muvvie Dovie" being his favorite until his father suggested he take it all a little more seriously.

And so, to Shaver, Dovie became "Mother Bird." Somehow it seemed more fitting than he knew, for the loving heart in the bouncing, chattering body spread its wings generously to include the love-starved boy. Two new "aunts" wrapped him in tenderness and affection.

Even more, the sisters opened their home to him. It was decided that Shaver should take on the responsibility of the Snodgrass farm. Under his father's direction and Anna's guidance, the young man felt perfectly capable of this step into maturity and welcomed it.

"Just think," he said rapturously, to the delight of his new aunts. "Teatime every day—and scones!"

27

WITH THE HOUSE BRIGHT AND SHINING AROUND her, from cellar to attic, Meredith stepped into the one room needing special attention: the kitchen.

It hadn't been easy. As the days and weeks had slipped away, mostly in a haze of weariness and humiliation, Meredith's accomplishments had steadily mounted, and with them her satisfaction.

True to form, her defeats and victories had been cataloged until every pocket, many drawers, and numerous writing pads had been filled with her lists and "household hints."

*Linens should not be folded, but rather rolled.

*Wood ashes made into a paste will scour knives and forks and keep them free of rust.

*Spread an old sheet on the floor over the rug before sewing, to catch threads.

*Never ever throw away old sheets. Tear them into bandages or dustcloths.

*Put brown paper on a cut to prevent bleeding.

*Soak blood stains in cold water before putting in hot water.

*Save old toothbrushes for cleaning and scrubbing small items.

*Put dishwater (sans soap) onto plants.

*Put ashes down toilet.

*Brown paper soaked in vinegar may be applied to

temples at night to prevent wrinkles. (This is a ridiculous untruth and does not work!)

*Do not boil tortoise shell combs!

*To whiten porcelain, boil peeled potatoes in it.

*Do not get any yolk in egg whites if you wish to make meringue.

*Dried apples need to be soaked in water overnight if they are not to resemble rubber in a pie.

*To prevent lamp wicks from smoking, soak them in vinegar. (Dry thoroughly to avoid humiliation when attempting to light.)

*IMPORTANT! Ammonia, inhaled, tends to take one's breath away, making one reel and faint into any arms that are available.

All these and many more Meredith studied and restudied, at times burning with some remembered embarrassment, at times glowing with pride over a task well done.

That she could "glow" at all was a major accomplishment in itself. One afternoon, more glowering than glowing, sniffing rather than smiling, burning rather than blessing, she had crept once more to the side of the gentle Gran, once again resting her flushed face on the blanketed knee. No words were necessary; the wise woman simply laid a twisted hand on the springing auburn hair and brushed it back tenderly.

"I've done it again, Gran. I got busy and forgot about the bread rising in the pans!"

"It's fallen flat, hasn't it?"

"Yes," Meredith admitted, adding grimly, "and ran all over the edges onto the warming oven."

"It's not the end of the world."

"But it's the end of the bread. I suppose I can rescue some of it and make fried bread. Again!"

"Bannock. I've made lots of it."

"Have you, Gran? What kept you at it—did you ever

feel like giving up—only you were too proud to admit defeat?"

In answer, Gran reached for the Bible usually sitting at her elbow. Gnarled fingers scrabbled among the thin leaves until she found a well-marked selection.

"Who can find a virtuous woman?" the old voice read. "For her price is far above rubies. The heart of her husband doth safely trust in her. . . . She will do him good and not evil all the days of her life."

"The heart of her husband . . ." Meredith repeated in a thoughtful whisper, while wheels turned and bells rang somewhere in the depths of her being.

Her motivation, she saw quite clearly, had been all wrong.

With Gran waiting patiently, Meredith drew the gold locket-watch from the bosom of her dress, snapped open the locket side, and studied the imperious, self-confident face. A man in a man's world, never seriously thwarted in any way, raised in luxury and inheriting a position of command, Emerson Brandt faced the world, his world, in near ignorance of what life was all about.

What was more, he had come near to hanging the same albatross of superciliousness about her neck.

"Oh, Gran!" Meredith half-moaned, half-laughed. "I've been such an ignoramus!"

"But very teachable," Gran included softly.

"So proud!"

"But taking humiliation in stride," defended Gran.

"Such a prig!"

"Always getting up and going on again, no matter the setback."

"And do you know why, Gran?"

"Something to do with that face—that man—in the locket."

"Everything to do with him! You see, Gran, he coolly concluded that I was no more fit to run an office than I was to run his household, although he was willing to give me a try on the latter after I became *adroit* enough at—"

"Adroit?" Gran inserted.

"Proficient, I suppose he meant. He said—," Meredith paused, "—I would be challenged by the prospect.

"So I took on the project," she continued thoughtfully, "for entirely the wrong reason. What you just read," and her head nodded in the direction of the Bible, "spelled it out for me. What I've done, I've done for the wrong reason, and never so that the heart of my husband might safely trust in me."

"Emerson?"

"It won't be Emerson, Gran. Someone—else, someone it makes me pleased to serve. Someone it gives me happiness to do things for."

Gran's touch was knowing, her silence just as knowing.

"What else does it say, Gran?" Meredith asked eventually.

"It says she will do him—her husband—good and not evil—she works willingly with her hands—rising while it is night, to give food to her household—"

Meredith nodded slowly, living it out, early rising by early rising.

"It says," Gran continued, "she girds herself with strength . . . her lamp does not go out at night . . . she spins and sews and clothes her household well. It says her husband is respected at the city gates where he sits among the elders of the land."

"He *would* be," Meredith agreed, "with such a partner."

"Such a woman is clothed with strength and honor— she speaks wisely and kindly."

"So much yet to learn—," Meredith whispered.

"She looketh well to the ways of her household," Gran read, "and eateth not the bread of idleness—"

"Amen to that!"

"Her children rise up and call her blessed; her husband also, and he praiseth her," Gran read. "Charm is deceptive," she paraphrased, "and beauty doesn't last, but a woman who fears the Lord is to be praised."

"Now *that*, Gran," Meredith said, as thoughtful as she had ever been in her young life, "is a challenge."

"Enough to last a lifetime," the voice of experience agreed.

"Gran," Meredith asked in a low, earnest voice, "would you pray with me? That's the kind of woman I want to be."

What followed was, in its way, a dedication ceremony. The challenge was outlined and accepted, the pledge was made, and the course of one life changed forever.

If Gran, head lifted above the bowed one, caught a glimpse of a dark face lit by some inner light before it withdrew into the shadowed hall, she, in her great wisdom, never mentioned it.

* * *

Meredith lifted the rag rug from in front of the kitchen range, took it outside, shook it, and left it on the fence to air. Back inside the kitchen, about to remove the ashes from the stove in which the fire had been allowed to die out, Meredith paused.

"Aha!" she crowed and threw several tea towels over the table and open shelves, wisely covering the food and dishes and supplies.

About to tackle cleaning the firebox, "Aha!" she murmured spontaneously again and pulled a pair of Dickson's heavy gloves onto her hands. "No burns today!"

The tray was carefully removed, carried out, and emptied—where it should have been. Aha!

The area under the oven was scraped with a piece of metal affixed to a long wire handle; this accumulation fell into a pail, and it too was taken to the proper repository.

"Jennie would be so proud of me," Meredith thought, well pleased with herself.

The stove lids on the back part of the range were lifted and the ashes below studied; only some were removed, a layer being left for protection in case a large flame from the firebox swept up the chimney, threatening to warp the top of the oven. Aha!

Making a sudsy pan of water from the reservoir's still-warm supply, Meredith reached energetically up into the high warming oven to wash that area thoroughly. Utensils stored around and on the back of the stove were washed.

The greasy splatters on the stove back were a challenge. Strong soap and what Jennie called "lots of elbow grease" did the job.

Since the stovetop was still warm, kerosene with brick dust would not be used to clean it. (Echoes of Jennie's shriek, which had stopped her from this procedure previously, lingered in the air.) Today Meredith wiped the stove with a rag dipped in cold coffee. Just realizing the coffee had not been thrown, willy-nilly, into the slops was enough to raise Meredith's chorus of "Ahas" to a crescendo.

Let Emerson Brandt top that! And with the thought, Meredith's belligerence toward the absent Emerson fizzled out, never to appear again.

Meredith's final "Aha!" was for that particular triumph. And it was that "Aha!" that was heard by Dickson Gray.

"Now what was that all about?" he asked mildly, stepping into the kitchen, Jennie at his heels.

"Just finishing up a big job," Meredith explained quickly. And with a "Watch this, Miss Jennie" look in her eye, she took the heavy cast iron teakettle, its bottom black from sitting over an open flame, marched with it to the plowed ground at the edge of the garden plot, set it down, and turned it around and around, thus scouring off the black soot. Rinsing it at the well, Meredith took it inside and set it—as proudly as though it were an elegant samovar in a Russian palace—on her shining range.

"What's for supper, Aunt Meredith?" a duly impressed Jennie asked.

Meredith's face fell. With all the day's triumphs, she had forgotten to leave a kettle of stew or beans simmering, to be reheated when the stove was lit again. Challenges, it seemed, would indeed last a lifetime.

"Bannock, for one thing," she told the child, adding when she saw the crest-fallen face, "or how about johnnycake—with some of this golden syrup you just brought from the store?"

A happy Jennie went to take the mail to Gran. While Dickson lit the fire in the range, Meredith began assembling johnnycake ingredients.

"Corn meal—flour—same amounts. Half teaspoon salt—six teaspoons baking powder—two eggs—" With astonishment, Meredith realized she had proceeded without the customary slip of paper to guide her every step.

"Aha!" she exulted under her breath and turned to catch an unguarded expression on Dickson's face. If she hadn't known better, she would have identified it as admiration.

Meredith glanced down at herself; she hadn't removed the soot-soiled apron, her tumbled hair tickled her cheek, and a quick glance in the small washstand mirror revealed a smudge on her nose. Removing the grimy apron, tucking her hair, and scrubbing her nose, Meredith concluded she had made the mistake of her life. Admiration indeed!

By a hand thrust experimentally into the oven she judged the heat just right, thrust in the pan of johnnycake, and slammed the oven door. She felt flushed with pleasure over her accomplishments.

Turning from the stove, she saw Dickson pull a letter from his pocket and hold it uncertainly.

"I received this today—from Miss Janoski," he said. And Meredith's heart seemed to stand still.

"She's ready to come," she acknowledged simply.

"She'll come upon receiving word from me that the position is still open."

"Of course you must write her," Meredith said, turning to the table and fumbling among the eggshells with fingers that—strangely—were trembling.

"Must I?" Dickson's voice was gentle.

"It would solve your problems very nicely." Meredith crushed the eggshells in her hand and never felt the sharp edges.

"My problems?"

"Fallen bread—bitter coffee—tough pastry—scorched shirts."

"You haven't heard me complaining, have you?" Dickson asked, again in that gentle tone.

Meredith was silent, but her heart was swelling with the wonder of the realization—never had this man grumbled or complained; neither had he scorned or belittled. And neither had Gran, the teacher at whose knee Meredith had begun to learn true values. And neither had little Jennie; even her advice had been given kindly. The thought of what Meredith had found here, in this simple backwoods home, shook her profoundly.

"You've all been very—kind," she said thickly.

"It would make me—us—very happy if you stayed." Dickson stepped to Meredith's side, put his hands on her shoulders, and turned her toward him.

"Is there any—chance?" Dickson's eyes were very dark indeed. "Do you understand what I'm asking, Meredith?"

For the space of a dozen heartbeats Meredith looked deeply into Dickson's eyes. What she saw there was enough to cause her to draw a deep breath and respond simply, "Yes."

Dickson's grip loosened and his hands dropped. "That's enough—for now," he said simply.

Dickson's long legs took him across the kitchen. Strangely atremble, Meredith leaned back against the table, unaware that the slight jar was enough to set the extra eggs, left carelessly loose on the table top, into a slow roll toward the edge—and the floor.

Just before the first one plopped and broke, Dickson passed through the door with one final comment.

It was, unmistakably, an exultant, triumphant "Aha!"

28

NEVER HAD THE LITTLE LOG HOUSE SHONE AS IT did now. Windows sparkled inside and out. Cupboards had been emptied and cleaned, bedding washed, rugs beaten. The cellar had been rearranged, cleaned, and restocked.

Finally, at the last, baking had been done. There would be a fresh supply of oat cakes for Moira. Bread filled the house with new-baked fragrance; the small table in the front room was set for tea.

Packing to go, Aunt Allis had presented Cassie with her own special Shetland shawl, made from a brilliant combination of black, blue, and cardinal yarns. For Robin she produced a pair of booties, secretly crocheted of zephyr yarn and as soft as dandelion seed.

Cassie clutched the treasures, swallowing down tears. Don't go! Don't go! she pleaded silently. Don't go and leave me with Lady Moira!

But it was a useless cry. Andrew would not return without Moira. Cassie could see the anticipation in his eyes and wept, wondering why she cried.

Though the weather was warm, Andrew took along a misty-fine white shawl lifted from Moira's dresser drawer, and Cassie's heart panged, and she didn't understand why.

The buggy was not yet out of sight, Aunt Allis waving and calling good-byes, when Cassie's decision was made. Without previous thought but feverishly necessary, she made the only decision she could—and couldn't fathom why. She only knew she had to be gone when Andrew returned with Moira—wrapped in his love and his carefully chosen shawl—at his side.

Although there was no need for hurry, it was with desperate haste she went through the house locating her things and packing them. Bit by bit she carried them to the covered shelter where the wagon was stored and lifted them in, panting with the exertion and straining with the effort.

Her boxes and goods stored in the shed were even more difficult; some she unpacked and carried piecemeal, struggling far beyond what was wise in her advanced pregnancy. But an undefined urgency drove her.

The sweet, familiar sounds of the homestead filled her ears with memories she would cherish forever; only half-seeing, her eyes recorded the dear sights that she couldn't bear the thought of leaving—and was driven to abandon. Stumbling, moving mindlessly, Cassie headed for the meadow and the oxen. Topping the small rise, she could see the slough and the cattle and horses grouped around it, some feeding on the abundant grasses, others recumbent, placidly chewing their cuds. Cassie moved among them; from one to another she passed, growing perplexed, eventually staring, almost wild-eyed, over the familiar animal shapes.

The oxen—Bib and Tucker—were gone.

Dropping to her knees in the grass, cradling her bulging body in her two arms, Cassie let the helpless tears fall.

"Andrew—Andrew—," she wept, anguished, knowing surely Andrew had forestalled her hurried exit from his life. "You don't know what you've done! And I can't tell you!"

Knowing she would have to see it through—the bitterness of being the bystander to the happiness and contentment of Andrew MacTavish and his cherished love—Cassie let the tears run.

"It's too much—I can't bear it!" she wept. "I need—I need arms stronger than mine—wisdom greater than mine. I need You, Father!"

All that, and more, Cassie found, crouching in wild grasses, turning—finally and fully—to the One who, she realized, had been her loving Companion since the moment she had first turned to Him in the desolation of her lonely wagon bed under the prairie stars. For had she not come to the One who invited, "Come unto me," and who promised, "I will sustain thee"?

With God true to His Word, as He always had been and always would be, the earnest seeker found grace to help in time of need. Cassie's eyes lifted to the blue expanse of the heavens as her tears dried in the warmth and wind of midday. Only then did she struggle to her feet and turn toward the house, knowing she could face the next few days and weeks and whatever pain they brought—and face them with peace.

"We'll make it through—now," she told the beloved bundle that seemed to press her down with every step.

Cassie's tears and torments were over when at last she heard the sound of an approaching rig. The dog, who accompanied Andrew everywhere, bounded out of the circling bush first, followed closely by the buggy.

With heart pounding but hand purposeful, Cassie poured hot water into the waiting teapot to warm it for the moment she would drop in the tea ball containing the proper measure of "Star of India"—a choice grade and Moira's favorite.

Lifting the best cups from the cupboard shelves to the table, she could hear Andrew's commands to the horse and the buggy's stop at the door of the lean-to. Through the small window she could see Andrew circle the rig and reach a hand to his companion. How small she was—how dainty! And how gracefully she stepped down, her head bent under a veiled hat that sat on her masses of hair like a crown on a regal head, her gloved hand held possessively by Andrew's firm grip.

Back pressed to the table, Cassie waited. Andrew opened the door, his eyes ablaze, his mouth soft with his smiling, his hand under the elbow of the woman stepping like a queen into her castle.

"Home!" the voice said with satisfaction.

And Cassie, with a full and willing heart, gave over into the arrival's hands the store of treasures she had—mistakenly, for a time—dreamed were her own.

"So this is Cassie," a pleasant voice said, and Cassie looked into the kindest eyes she had ever seen—kind eyes in a faded, sweet face.

Putting his arms around the fragile shoulders, Andrew said, "Cassie—this is Moira, my mother."

As a great roaring filled her ears, Cassie's knees gave way, and she toppled floorward. Only hazily, she felt Andrew's arms catch her, pick her up, stride with her toward the bedroom.

"Robin—," Cassie gasped and curled herself into a ball of pain under the quilt Andrew drew over her.

"No need tae unhitch, laddie," the pleasant voice said briskly. "Go for Anna. I'll take care of things her-r-re."

As she spoke, Moira MacTavish was unpinning her hat, removing her gloves, laying aside her shawl.

"I'll go and clean up a bit, lassie," she said comfortingly, "and make the tea. You'll have time, per-r-rhaps, for a cuppa befor-r-re things get serious.

"Ther-r-re, ther-r-re," she soothed, "no need tae cr-r-ry. All will be well . . ."

And Cassie was sure it would be.

* * *

At dawn the following morning, freshly gowned, her hair brushed back from a face lit with joy, spent, but happier than she could ever remember being, and with the night's travail but a memory, Cassie propped herself against her pillows and held out her arms to her baby, sweet and clean in her handmade garments and sound asleep.

It was Andrew who placed the babe—still curved in the position it had occupied for nine months in her mother's body—into the reaching arms.

It had been Andrew, waiting tensely outside the bedroom door through the long night hours, who had received the squirming, bawling scrap of humanity from Anna's capable hands, carrying it in triumph to the side of the kitchen range and his mother's practiced ministrations.

It was Andrew who cautioned now, "Careful, lass, dinna squeeze too tight!" and who had the grace to look a bit sheepish after he had said it.

It was Andrew who seated himself carefully alongside mother and babe, pulling back the shawl and toying softly with the downy fluff on the pink scalp.

It was Andrew who said the words that took Cassie's dreams and shaped them, at long last, into reality.

"I canna let you go, lass. Not ever."

It was in Andrew's arms, wrapping around her sweetly, possessively, and drawing her and the baby into the circle of his love, that Cassie found anchor—finally and gladly—in her desired haven.

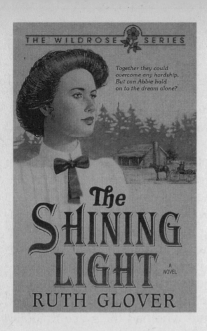

Together they could overcome any hardship, But can Abbie hold on to the dream alone?

THE SHINING LIGHT

Book One in
The Wildrose Series

Life in the big city was comfortable for Worth and Abbie Rooney. But as with so many others at the turn of the century, the promise of land and a new life in the West was a shining light that beckoned, illuminating hearts and imaginations.

For Worth it was simple: Sell! Move West! Homestead! For Abbie the issue was more difficult, though loyalty won—and she willingly embraced his dream as her own.

And indeed, Saskatchewan was verdant and lovely, a land to be prized. But it was also harsh. Even as it promised, it threatened. Worth and Abbie knew well that it would be a struggle to carve out this new existence in a territory where the summers were short and toilsome and the winters long and lonely. They also knew that together they could overcome any adversity. But can Abbie hold on to the dream alone?

Where is God's light when everything seems so dark?

THE SHINING LIGHT   **BF083-411-514X**

*Purchase from your favorite bookstore,
or order toll-free from:*
BEACON HILL PRESS OF KANSAS CITY
800-877-0700